Periphery
By Kelly E. Lindner

ISBN-13: 978-0615923987
ISBN-10: 0615923984

See all my books at KellyELindner.com.

Feathers

Sometimes I dream of my mother just before it happened. Her face barely touched with wrinkles and stress. Smile warm and eyes bright.

She stands with her back to the blue couch that sits against the front window—the really comfortable one stuffed with down feathers that she lies across while she reads. It's a strangely frozen moment, but I don't understand its significance. Then I hear smoking tires, yells and a loud stereo.

As bullets fly, I keep thinking, "but I wasn't home when it happened. I wasn't *there*." And that seems reflected in the strange faux memory, because despite what's apparently happening right before me, my eyes turn against my will. I watch the feathers explode from the couch as it's riddled with unforgiving metal, not my mom as she dies. She remains right where I can't see her. A bloody, convulsing blur. In my periphery.

The Sheriff's Daughter

"Will you walk me home?" asks a hopeful voice matched with likewise eyes. It's a pair I've never seen before, but that isn't too unusual. I go to a small high school, but I don't really pay attention to my classmates. I'm not really looking for friends. And it's also not unusual for me to get this question every now and then at the end of a school day.

I'm the sheriff's daughter. Even though I'm tiny and couldn't provide any physical protection, no one messes with me because of that. And we have an extreme bully problem at our school. Though this year, I admit it's gotten a little better.

"Sure," I say into the unfamiliar eyes, trying not to sound annoyed. I am a little. I wasn't in the mood for small talk. I'm not good at it.

This girl seems extremely sweet though. Her voice is airy and light, and she's even shorter than me, which is odd. I'm 5 ft. 3 in., and I can't help but notice that she's fairly pretty.

She has that perfect natural blonde hair (that's almost neon) and watery blue eyes. I have blonde hair as well, what they call dishwater blonde, and dark brown eyes I hate. I've always wanted blue eyes. At this moment, I hate her a little for her pretty hair and eyes. In fact, she's really pretty in general. So why would anyone mess with her? But then I instantly know the culprit.

"Travis is bothering you?" I ask as we start to walk.

"Yeah," she says, eyeing her feet.

How he hasn't gotten slapped with a date rape charge yet is beyond me. "I'm sorry about that," I say, not knowing what else to say.

"Yeah, it kinda sucks to get sexually harassed on your first day."

So she *is* new to Haven. I'm not totally antisocial for not noticing her before. "You haven't reported him?"

She just shakes her head. "Everyone told me I should just hang out with you."

This stops me. She stops walking too, startled by my reaction.

"Who's everyone?" I ask, sounding more irritated than I mean to.

"Everyone," she repeats like it's an answer. She can tell I'm still unsatisfied, so she adds, "*Literally everyone.*"

I'm unsure what to do with this strange information. I knew I had a reputation—I've seriously even had giant guys getting bullied by even bigger guys ask if I can walk them home before—but this girl wants to hang out with me to help protect her from

Travis?

Travis has never seemed particularly afraid of my dad. He's rich, privileged and doesn't really worry much about the law. His dad can buy him out of trouble. So why doesn't he ever mess with me? This isn't the first time I've asked myself this question. But it is the first time I haven't just dismissed it with, "Well, I'm the sheriff's daughter."

I try to move on in the conversation even though my mind is still totally hung-up.

"So this is just a friendship of convenience for you," I tease her.

Her face goes white, and she begins spitting apologies.

"I'm so sorry," she sputters nervously. "I never thought—"

I start laughing, which just confuses her more.

"It's okay," I tell her. "I'm *teasing* you." Then I give her a friendly soft punch in the shoulder that turns out awkward, which embarrasses me.

She stares at the place where my hand hit her shoulder. "That hurt," says the girl I just barely touched.

Geez. What a wuss.

But, still embarrassed, I apologize under my breath and change the subject.

"Sure, you can hang out with me," I tell her. Her face lights up. "It would actually be nice to have someone to talk to on a regular basis. You know, a lot of students avoid me," I admit, instantly regretting that I'm being so raw and open.

"It is kinda weird," she admits.

"Yeah," I agree.

It *is* kinda weird.

Morgan, as it turns out she's called, wants to meet my father, undoubtedly to see what all the fuss is about. We stop at my Victorian-style, two-story house first on the way to hers, which is apparently just a few streets away. When we walk in and see my dad lying back in his easy chair, still in uniform, watching the football game, I can see from her expression that this has done nothing to slake her expectations.

Though my father is certainly muscular and compact, he's also only 5 ft. 10 in. and always cracking jokes and doing whatever he can to put a person at ease. His off-duty personality is extremely unintimidating. Sure, he's a little different with his game-face on, and he is undoubtedly strong enough to do someone some damage.

When he was younger and not a policeman yet, two large men tried to jump him when he walked away from an ATM. He beat them both into crying, bloody messes. They looked like they had been beaten with a police baton, but no weapon was found. He got so angry he doesn't even remember doing this, but those guys, and just about everyone in the entire city, never messed with him again.

It definitely had an impact on him becoming sheriff in the future. (He also had a good slogan: "Rob Janus will put the 'safe' back in Haven.") Even though it was something like five years ago, everyone knows the story. But this isn't something you can guess by just looking at him. He's shorter than most of the guys on our football team.

I can tell that Morgan is threading a similar line of thought. She's wondering, "What's so scary about this guy?"

Exactly.

I'm having an outline of a thought, but I can't even give it a voice inside my head.

"Dad, this is Morgan," I tell him.

"Hi, Morgan!" he says as he jumps to his feet and extends his hand. "It's always a pleasure to meet one of Lana's friends who doesn't know better yet," my dad jokes.

Morgan cringes from my dad's crushing handshake; he literally doesn't know his own strength. I can't help giving him a little punch in the arm for his comment.

"Owww," he jokes, though I know my weak little punch has no effect on him.

"So you're both freakishly strong," Morgan says so dryly I can barely tell she's being sarcastic.

"No, just him," I correct her. But my father's smile falls a little.

"Lana can certainly be strong when she needs to be," my father says. I really think he's just trying to make me feel better about myself.

I laugh off his encouragement with a "whatever," and it's easy to move on from the gushy moment—for me anyway.

Morgan looks hung up on his statement for some reason. The way she looks at us in general makes me think she finds us oddly fascinating, and I really don't understand why. We're completely average.

Somehow my overly friendly father talks Morgan into staying for dinner. She's excited by his infectiously social demeanor. I don't really argue but really wasn't in the mood to share my dinner table with a girl I barely know.

But my dad loves it when I make friends, and honestly he sometimes makes better friends with people my age than I do.

There have been times when guys I had a crush on have come over after school and asked, "Is your dad here? I thought we could watch the game."

Ugh.

But that is something to consider. The kids my age don't really seem to be afraid of my father. It's really all the adults in town who treat him in that careful way—the way that all the kids in town...well...never mind.

My dad is also an amazing cook, which Morgan soon learns when she bites into the stuffed bell peppers he somehow had the time to put together after work, from scratch.

"This is really good," she says with true sincerity.

"Well, thank you very much," my dad says in his charming Southern drawl. It's the other reason my dad is so popular with the hungry, growing boys of my school—the ones who act like they'll faint if they don't eat huge meals every two hours. Sometimes they just invite themselves over by asking, "So what's your dad cooking tonight?"

With all these kids in and out of my house to see my dad, you'd think I'd be more popular. Not really.

"You're welcome to join us anytime," he tells Morgan, but he's not just being polite. He means it.

Great. I'm never getting rid of this girl. But at least she seems legitimately nice. So I decide to attempt small talk, which I seldom do.

"So, Morgan, what brings you to Haven?"

"My dad's business," she says, forking a whole lot more stuffed pepper into her mouth.

"He must be the one who brought in the car dealership," Dad deduces quickly. "From California, right? Mac Nelson?"

"Yes," Morgan says, impressed, since they probably haven't been in town long, but my dad makes all major changes about his town his business.

He takes his role very seriously, and so far that's been a good thing for Haven. It wasn't the safest place when we first moved here. Once my dad became sheriff, though, he did some major cleanup.

"So where is Mrs. Janus tonight?" Morgan asks, which causes my dad to drop his fork with a loud clank that makes everything suddenly awkward.

He stares at his plate while I slip Morgan a warning look that I instantly feel guilty about. She's probably the only person in town who doesn't know that story yet, and why would she?

My mom's death happened right after my dad started to

clean up the town. After that, my dad was determined to do an even better job. The bad element is almost completely driven out now. *Almost.*

I see Morgan panic. She catches on before he answers her.

"She passed away," my father says gently, without meeting her eyes or smiling (which is odd for him) before picking up his escaped fork and taking another bite of stuffed pepper.

It isn't long, though, before he's back to his usual social self, but it takes a subject change from me to kick him back into gear.

"Well, Dad, we should see if we can get me a discount on a car from Morgan's dad," I say hopefully.

"*Right,*" he laughs. "*That'll happen.*"

"Well, I'll be 16 in a few months," I say.

"Ha. Try 18," he says sternly.

Morgan shoots me a thankful look.

It isn't long before it's completely dark outside, and Morgan's house is still a few blocks away.

"Lana, why don't you walk Morgan home?" Dad suggests. I get to my feet instantly.

"But then she'll have to walk back here by herself," Morgan objects.

"She'll be fine," Dad says, not even meeting her eyes when he brushes off her concern. My safety hasn't been something he's concerned himself with since my mother died, which is really strange. You'd think he'd become a hyper-worrier after an experience like that.

On the way to her house, Morgan apologizes profusely for "stepping in it" about my mom, but I tell her several times not to worry about it.

"Seriously, how could you know?" I assure her very strongly on about time number six. "No one told you."

I am surprised no one at school mentioned it to her, though I guess it's about 2-years-old news by now.

"What happened?" she pushes, like everyone always does eventually.

"She was killed in a drive-by when we first moved here," I tell her. I know the phrase "drive-by" probably sounds really strange to someone new to Haven.

"What?" she asks.

"Haven didn't used to be the safest place," I say to her shocked face.

"But it is now," she realizes when she composes herself. "Because of your dad....the *teddy bear*," she jokes.

It's probably the first joke she's attempted, and it's pretty funny.

"Yeah, he's not like that when he works," I tell her with a laugh. "He can be all business, and the adults in town do not cross him. He took down some major drug lords when he became sheriff, and those were some powerful people. He's not afraid of anyone."

"It must be true, but I just don't see how anyone could be afraid of him," she says.

I've always struggled with this myself, but he is my father. I have no reason to fear him.

"And actually," Morgan continues. "All the kids at school go on and on about how friendly and nice he is. They don't seem intimidated at all."

"He's different with kids. He gives them a little leeway— well, *most* anyway. He can usually tell right away which kids are good or bad. He's not very fond of Travis, for instance," I tell her.

He actually has some really bizarre suspicions about both Travis and his dad. The ones about Travis are mostly likely true, but the ones about Travis's father....

Even I believe he's grasping at straws.

"Good taste," she says with a laugh.

"Yeah."

I realize we've been standing on her doorstep talking for the last few minutes. I look up to see a brand new house that's probably three times the size of mine. Makes sense with the whole dealership thing, I suppose.

Her father opens the front door and peers at us, tired and a little annoyed.

"Time to come in now, Morgan," he says. Then he gives me a strange look. "You must be the sheriff's daughter."

And apparently I have no name outside of that these days.

"Yes, I'm Kalana Janus," I correct him.

He doesn't seem to notice.

"Your father called and told me you were walking Morgan home," he tells me, a little friendlier now. "I appreciate it."

Of course he did.

"No problem. Welcome to the neighborhood," I say with an awkward wave, trying to sound warm.

"Well, thank you," he says with a smile. "Morgan?"

She goes inside on command, and I begin the short, but dark, trek home. Even before my father cleaned up this town, he let me walk these streets alone. They were different streets then, very dangerous, but for some reason it didn't bother him much.

That leads to the thought I've been pushing away for some

time. My father has never been remotely concerned about my safety. All the adults in town are afraid of my father—even the good ones that have no reason to fear him—so they'd never mess with me. But all the kids in town, who all agree that my dad is a lot of fun and a good cook, aren't afraid of him at all. They're afraid of...me.

Why?

The only strange thing about me is the cutting. And though I'm sure fellow students have guessed that about me from my occasionally non-weather-appropriate clothing, I doubt any of them actually know about it for sure.

I barely know about it myself, though it is strange that the first episode was the night my mom was killed.

While our front room was sprayed with bullets, I should've just been getting home from school, but I wasn't there.

I was found two hours later facedown on someone's lawn, with slashed wrists, nowhere near my usual walking route. There was nothing sharp anywhere near me.

I remember leaving school to walk home, but the rest is blank, until I woke up in the emergency room to Dad telling me Mom was dead.

Emergency Room

I wake in my bed and smell blood. I know the source without having to guess. I draw my wrists to my eyes to find them slashed, again. I fell asleep watching TV pretty early tonight but wake up like this. And it isn't the first time. It's more like the fourth. But it's been at least six months since the last incident.

I stumble to my father's room, and without a word, he takes me to the town emergency center, where they're used to me showing up like this. It hasn't happened *that* many times, but it's certainly been more than once. I even have the same nurse as usual, who injects me with the local anesthesia even before the doctor arrives since this is so routine.

Even though she's been my nurse several times now, I've never noticed how blue her eyes are—like Elijah Wood's—so blue they're creepy —or maybe it's just the way she has them locked on me, like she's in awe of me or something. Or maybe she just thinks I'm a freak too.

Dr. Menzer arrives, dismisses the nurse and begins stitching me up without a word.

Dr. Menzer is always pretty calm. It's not just that he's desensitized because he's a doctor; it's just his personality. He usually appears half-asleep, or bored.

I'm certainly not bored. I never get over how strange being numb from my forearms to my wrists feels because of local anesthesia. I don't feel pain, but I feel the tugging of the small wire through my skin.

"So it's just sleepwalking again?" I ask him.

"Yep," he says. "Most people have a chemical released in their brains that keeps them paralyzed during REM sleep. You don't."

This isn't new information. He's told me this before.

"But why do I always slash my wrists?"

"Sleepwalkers tend to do repeated actions. Maybe you think you're chopping vegetables or something."

It's anything but a clean cut, so I wouldn't be too surprised if I was trying to cut something clumsily in my sleep, but I don't tend to chop things when I'm awake, or cook...*anything*.

"So you don't think I'm trying to hurt myself?"

My dad appears in the room, which seems to distract Dr. Menzer for a minute, and then he simply says, "No."

It seems a little too dismissive. It's a valid question even though it doesn't really make sense.

I have no desire to hurt myself, but who knows what sleepwalking Kalana is thinking, aside from aspiring to be a chef, *apparently*. I've never understood her.

"So you don't think I need to see a therapist?"

There's an exchange of eyes in the room, but they're all impassive, except mine. I'm pretty freaked.

"No," Dr. Menzer practically huffs before leaving the room.

"You're all good," he says over his shoulder. "Keep it clean."

"You don't think I need to see a therapist?" I ask my dad in the car on the way home, breaking the otherwise total silence.

He thinks for a minute and then says, "No, I don't think so," in the same submissive tone as Dr. Menzer.

"Why not? Is it about money? Are you embarrassed to have me go?"

He sighs. "No, Kalana. You just don't need one. You're a sleepwalker. Sleepwalkers do weird things. Dr. Menzer has upped your Clonazepam dosage, and that's really all we can do. You know your mother was a sleepwalker too."

"Yeah," I sigh. I do.

She never slashed her own wrists though.

She used to sleepwalk all over town, even before it was safe. It's amazing the types of people who used to be out at night in this town never hurt her *then*, when she was completely out of it.

But she looked pretty creepy with her wide, asleep dark eyes and flowy white nightgown, bordering on ethereal and ghostly at the same time. She was a scary sight to behold with her almost white, blonde hair.

I had to go find her a few times myself when my dad was out on patrol. I couldn't leave her out there alone, like a lost wandering child. She had no idea where she was. One time when I found her, she wasn't alone. Mr. Malone, Travis's dad, was there too. It was actually kind of odd. When I walked up, he was standing so close to her face it seemed he was about to kiss her, but when he saw me, he drew back. I decided it must've been my imagination.

"Mr. Malone?" I called when I saw him.

"Hello, Kalana," he said guiltily. "I was just about to escort your mother home."

"I can do it," I said, before I took her hand and guided her home like a stumbling toddler.

Mr. Malone certainly didn't seem to have any intention of hurting her that night. That's why I've never quite believed my dad's weird theories about him.

"And she did a lot of weird stuff," Dad continues. "And she tried seeing a therapist, going to sleep specialists...it just all leads to dead-ends. This is just the way you are."

It's disappointing to hear. Always waking up the same way, the rare times it does happen, is scary. What if next time I bleed out in my sleep?

It's like my dad heard my thoughts. "I can start watching over you as you sleep again if you want."

There was a time that this was a little more frequent that my dad sat in the uncomfortable wooden desk chair in my room to make sure I didn't hurt myself, but he had stopped the last six months because there hadn't been any incidents. We both kinda thought it was over.

"I just feel bad about you sitting up all night."

"It's not a problem," he says.

It does make me feel better. I sleep well the rest of the night knowing my dad is watching over me.

Blood Stains

Though our town is mostly cleaned up, our school is not without the occasional tragedy. I can tell there's been one today before I even hear about it. When I walk into school the next morning, the halls are quiet. When I move by the cafeteria, I see that the doors are closed, and the windows are blacked out. I can't even peer inside.

It isn't long before Morgan gloms on to me.

"Someone's died?" I ask before she can speak, but it's more of a statement.

"Yeah, last night," she says. "A kid was torn apart in the cafeteria."

Now *that* is new. Most of the deaths in this town involve knife wounds, gunshots or simply being beaten death. But torn apart?

"They said he was shredded. Like *really* shredded. Like pieces of him everywhere. I've heard they're still...cleaning."

"Who was it?"

"Tommy Mitchell?" she says, waiting for me to fill her in.

"One of Travis's best friends," I inform her.

That's also unusual, especially when you consider the history of deaths at this school. This might be the first time it's happened to someone who deserved it.

Tommy Mitchell was a horrible person. He beat up anyone who was gay or scrawny or disabled, and he, like the other two boys who have disappeared this year (presumably escaped to Mexico), were all linked to an unsolved murder.

They were all there the night Billy Engel was beaten to death about a year ago. They all claim they weren't, but my dad knows better. He questioned each one several times only to come up with frustratingly confident and smart-ass answers in addition to expensive and effective lawyers while parents cried themselves into denial.

But an anonymous eyewitness put five boys from our school there in the parking lot that night, beating poor Billy to death just because he had Down Syndrome and they thought it was fun.

One of them, Blaine Spencer, presumably fled the country the night of the murder, while another, Preston Owen, was thought to do the same several months later. And now one of the remaining three is dead. The two left are Rodney Chutney and Travis Malone.

I end up whispering all this to Morgan's white face in English class.

"You think someone's getting revenge?" she asks.

I just shrug, but it seems likely.

"With a giant *woodchipper*?" she asks with disbelief.

I'm not sure what to say. Yes, that part is certainly odd. How does one shred someone? But what's really strange is that the silence around the school today isn't remorse—it's guilt. The others feel guilty that they're glad he's gone. I certainly feel happy with no guilt whatsoever myself.

As I examine the faces of the students casually overhearing our conversation, I can see it's true.

"I guess so."

That day Morgan and I skip PE and sneak behind the gym to sit in the grass and watch the boy's soccer team practice, which is much better than suffering through dodgeball.

She inevitably asks me about Billy Engel. I tell her as much as I can, but it's a painful subject.

Billy was such a wonderful person. He had perfect pitch so they used him like a human tuning fork in choir; he really loved animals and often went with his brother to pet the lonely, unadopted cats at the Humane Society.

And he loved cars. He always carried a collection of matchbox cars he was really proud of.

He had one in every color of what he called the "good" kinds: a cherry Ferrari, mustard Lamborghini, gunmetal gray Mercedes, powder-blue Corvette, golden DeLorean and an ink-black Porsche.

I know because he showed me his collection every day like it was the first time I'd seen it. But I didn't mind.

Aside from being unbelievably sweet, Billy was one of the only people who didn't treat me like some kind of freak. He's the one who gave me the necklace I always wear tucked inside my shirt so no one can see. It's this strange silver charm of an angel stabbing some kind of reptilian demon with a staff. Billy said he found it in the street one night and it reminded him of me. Sweetness just runs in the Engel family, I guess.

He didn't deserve what happened to him. No one deserves that, but he *especially* didn't. The thought of anyone hurting him just makes me—

I swallow hard while explaining an edited version of this to Morgan, feeling as though I might throw up, and she looks horribly concerned, but the moment passes.

"What happened to him?" she asks when she feels safe from being spewed on.

"His brother got stuck doing a double shift and was late picking him up when his afterschool program let out. He was up here by himself waiting in the parking lot, and for some reason, Travis and all his cronies were still up here too, even though football practice had ended way before that. It's like they were waiting for him." I take a slow breath. "And then they took a golf club and beat him to death."

Morgan looks as sick as I felt just a moment ago. I see horror in her eyes when she realizes this is the school she now goes to. One where special children get beaten to death by jocks and they just get to walk around like nothing happened.

"How do you know that?" Morgan asks. "Were you there?"

"Someone was. An anonymous eyewitness gave all their names to my dad and told him what happened."

To this day, my dad still hasn't told me who. He's kept his word of protecting this fearful person who doesn't wish to be identified as the one who fingered some of the richest kids in school for a collective murder.

It's admirable really, though sometimes I wonder if my dad is the eyewitness himself so he can prosecute them without feeling the heat. Not that it'll work anyway.

"And two of the boys have disappeared?" she asks.

"Yes."

"Well, that's pretty guilty behavior."

"Yep."

Then Morgan eyes my elbow-length, knit, fingerless gloves, and this knowledge comes into her eyes that I wouldn't have expected so early. I guess she's more observant than I thought. Or she's just paid attention to what people are saying.

"So what's up with the gloves? It's practically still summer here."

"I'm just trying something," I lie with a dismissive shrug.

She doesn't buy it in the slightest, but it's not something I'm going to discuss with a girl I barely know, or anyone, outside my dad. And we don't even talk about it much.

It's then that a soccer ball barrels between us, and it isn't long before one of the players parts from the pack to retrieve it.

When I see who's approaching us with a warm smile, I feel instantly hot.

It's Tobias Engel, Billy's brother. He and his brother never really looked much alike. Tobias is tall, skinny but muscular, and has messy, straw-colored hair with bright green eyes. Billy had a much larger build. It was often even hard for me to believe they were related, except for a rare gentleness they shared.

Since the incident, I've talked to Tobias as little as possible. Not because I don't like him, but because I *do*. For some reason, liking him has made me feel guilty about Billy's death, even though that doesn't remotely make sense. It's not like *I* killed him.

But Tobias has never allowed me to avoid him. He takes every opportunity to talk to me. He thinks I'm some kind of saint for always hanging with his brother the way I did. We often all hung out together, and back then his closeness didn't bother me, but now it would just feel tainted by sadness.

I even feel uneasy in his warm presence right now, but I try to be friendly because I know what a great person he is.

"Hi, Kalana," he says, his eyes full of a light I don't understand. (I'm not much to look at compared to him.) "Skipping PE, I see."

"Yeah," I admit with a sigh. "While you're excelling at sports," I tease. He's good at just about everything—sports included.

To my surprise, he throws the ball back to his teammates and sits down with us.

"I haven't seen you around much lately," he says, but not in an accusatory way. He's not like that. It's more of an observation.

"Well, outside school I don't do much," I admit and then mentally add, "outside of visiting the emergency room way too often."

"Yeah, I've noticed that," he says softly, seeming sad. It makes me try too hard to distract him.

"Have you met Morgan?" I say with too much enthusiasm in both my voice and my gesture. But she seems pleased to be introduced, maybe a little too much so.

"No, I haven't," he says warmly, turning to her. "Morgan, I'm Tobias," he says paired with a warm handshake.

"Nice to meet you," she coos in her perfectly sweet voice. Even though I started this chain of events I suddenly want to strangle her. Why does she have to be so pretty and cute? But they'd go together nicely. They're both adorable and sweet. Maybe I shouldn't stand in the way. No. I still want to strangle her.

"Well, Kalana," he says, turning his attention back to me, which is both wonderful and seemingly impossible at the same time. "I hope I see you around more. You know you can come over or call anytime. I mean, you still have my number, right?"

"Yes," I say, feeling like a horrible friend. I've just neglected to use it for the last year....

"Well, seriously. Don't be afraid to use it. I've been dying to catch up with you. You know, I really miss you," he says, his words so nakedly honest I want to run into his arms crying about what a horrible person I've been, avoiding him just for my own comfort.

"I've really missed you too, Tobias," I admit, fighting tears.

I feel Morgan's eyes weighing on me in surprise.

Don't get too excited. That's as gushy as I get.

Tobias returns to his soccer pack, and Morgan continues to stare at me while I refuse to meet all the questions in her eyes.

"He really likes you," she says when he's safely out of earshot.

"I know," I sigh, eyeing the grass.

"And you like him too," she puts together easily. "Why do you avoid him?"

"Because he's too good for me."

"I don't think that's true."

"He deserves someone more like you. You're both so *good*."

"Yeah, well, he seems to already know what he wants," she says teasingly.

"Yeah, but *why*?"

"You have mirrors at your house, right?" Morgan jokes. I know I'm not horrible looking, but it's patronizing for someone as naturally gorgeous as Morgan to try and convince me I'm pretty. I glare at her.

"Yeah, well, I'm a mess," I say, trying not to eye the black gloves wrapped around my pitch-black secret. I'm sure Morgan doesn't have any of those. Her secrets are probably more like a dark shade of pink. Her eyes land on the gloves as well but pull away quickly.

"I don't think he'd care," she says but then quickly adds, "about *whatever's* wrong," like she doesn't already have a clue. "He'd probably just want to help you."

Damn it. She has heard the rumors, but she's trying to bait me into telling her myself so she doesn't have to ask the awkward question: "Do you cut yourself?" Well, screw that.

"Well, that's even worse," I say. Then my tone becomes pointed with a not-so-subtle dual meaning. "I don't want him to try and save me and realize I'm beyond help."

"You're not beyond help," she objects confidently, like she could even know.

I just shake my head at her in frustration.

"And even if you were, I don't think that would bother him," she claims.

She has no idea what she's talking about. She barely knows

him, and she certainly doesn't know me. But I have to admit, if anything, that certainly makes her objective.

"You should see him," Morgan pushes, giving me an unexpected and playful nudge with one shoulder. I can't help laughing at her implausible optimism.

"It just feels too weird."

"You should see him *tonight*," Morgan insists with so much encouragement in her voice it's annoying, or possibly affecting.

I leave when school lets out convinced that I won't go see Tobias simply because Morgan pressured me to. But then I somehow end up on his doorstep, ringing his doorbell with a shaky hand.

When he opens the door, his face lights up in that familiar way I just don't get. Then, before either of us can say hi, he opens the screen door and pulls me up three concrete steps into his arms, like I'm weightless. It's simultaneously awkward and wonderful.

"You came!" he breathes into my ear.

When he releases me, our faces seem way too close, but he doesn't seem to remotely notice or mind. I'm not sure which. I'm also very aware that our arms are still hung loosely around each other's bodies, with our legs tangled together.

"Yeah," I say weakly. "And I'm so sorry I haven't made it over in a while…or *called*," I squeak out.

When I hear myself add that last part, I know there's no excuse for my behavior. It's his brother that died, and I left him alone in that, because I selfishly didn't want to see him in pain. I'm a monster.

"It's okay, Kalana," he assures me with his eyes drilling straight into mine, with seemingly no plans of retreating from that intimate place.

He's all about eye contact. I won't be able to hide anything. He's always told me my eyes were really expressive, though he's the only one who seems to think so. I forgot about his natural intuition for my feelings. It's part of the reason I've stayed away.

"It's not," I say, hating myself. "You needed me this year, and I wasn't there."

"And you needed to be by yourself," he excuses me too easily, like always. "That's how you are. I understand."

Tears pile in my eyes. "But I just wish I wasn't like that."

"But you are. And I like who you are. You should stay that way. And I'm so glad you're here," he says so warmly. I don't deserve it. I don't.

He leads me inside his house by the hand into the kitchen,

where his parents are eating dinner. His mom jumps from her chair; she's that excited to see me. My heart clenches painfully. Her eyes are still so warm yet minced with a sadness that's barely buried. For them, it's still a fresh wound.

"Kalana!" his mother says so excitedly I feel sick. "It's so wonderful to see you!"

"You too," I barely get out as lunch rises in my throat.

It gets even worse when I look at his dad's worn face. He struggles to smile but is still so sad he's unable to speak. He just nods. I feel dizzy.

"Well, please join us for dinner," Tobias's mom says politely, even though they're obviously practically finished.

I look at her hopeful face surrounded by her goddess-like curls. For a mom, she's very youthful. She's always felt impossibly close to my age, but it's just good genes, which, obviously, Tobias shares.

I so want to give her what she wants: To make small talk and then deeper conversation with someone who also misses her son and feels the pain she feels.

But I feel like my voice is suddenly completely inaccessible and I'm about to projectile vomit my stomach contents all over their kitchen.

"Mom, I sense Kalana's overwhelmed right now," Tobias gleans accurately, but I could hit him. They're the ones who've lost a son, and he's asking them to coddle me?

Jesus, Tobias! I pull away from him.

I'm going outside. I can't be here. I have to run. But Tobias senses this and doesn't accept it. He puts an arm tightly around my shoulders, holding me in place.

"Is it alright if we just hang in my room?" he asks them.

"Of course, honey," only his mom says. His dad seems like a shadow of his former self. I'm gonna be sick.

When he leads me to his room, I feel a wave of relief, and my stomach settles quickly.

It's nice to be in a place so familiar, though it's not really much to look at. Just a bed with a flannel comforter, a black guitar leaning against a wall, Muse posters and a laptop on a small, bare glass desk.

But it's Tobias's room. A place I've spent an inordinate amount of time in the past talking and laughing with Tobias and...and with Billy.

In some strange way, it's like coming home after being away for a long time. The year-long absence suddenly feels both invisible and more pronounced.

"So what do you want to do?" he asks, excitedly. He's already plugged his smartphone into the speakers on his desk, which means he has some more strange ambient techno to play for me, probably even a year's worth.

"I sense you have some stuff to play for me," I glean.

"I sure do. Pandora is my new favorite thing."

He presses a button, and the room floods with soothing and rhythmic sounds. I lay back on the bed like I've done a million times, and he lays the opposite way so our turned heads are parallel but our feet are on different ends of the bed. It's like we never let this strange ritual drop.

"Listen to this part," he says, excitedly drumming his knees.

"Yeah, it's good," I agree sincerely.

He has good taste. Something about the music he picks always makes me feel completely relaxed, like I'm weightless while my mind completely wanders. And it never seems to go anywhere unpleasant.

Right now I'm thinking about the last time we did this with Billy, and it isn't making me sad. It's a nice memory.

He was sitting on the floor throwing his arms around enthusiastically until he got up and started jumping around and throwing this arms excitedly, somewhat to the beat. He called it dancing. It wasn't really that similar. But he always did it so joyfully that Tobias and I would sit up and clap and cheer him on. He was such a fun person.

"Kalana, are you okay?" Tobias asks me, his concerned eyes suddenly on mine. His mouth so close I can feel his breath on my lips as he asks.

I don't understand until I touch my cheeks with my fingers to find them wet. I've been crying, and I didn't even feel the tears. "You're thinking about Billy, aren't you?" he asks. "The last time we were all here together?"

I push myself to nod but hardly accomplish the motion. Without a word, he kneels on the bed and pulls me into a hard hug with his cheek pressed against the dip of one shoulder. I flush.

Then he's crying too. His warm tears soak into the shoulder of my shirt. "I'm so glad you're back," he says in between sobs. "I've missed you so much."

When he walks me out a few hours later, he's as cheerful as ever, and it's dark now.

"I don't feel right about you walking home alone in the dark," he says after a quick look around.

"I'm fine," I say over my shoulder in a voice that's probably too hard, but I'm not remotely worried about walking the mere three blocks to my house. Neither is my dad, I'm certain. No one messes with the girl who goes crazy and cuts herself. And I'm sure it doesn't hurt that she's also the sheriff's daughter.

"I insist," he says, matching my pace as I move quickly to leave his property, hoping to encourage him to stay put, but it doesn't work. But it's nice to have him still near me as I walk home.

I wasn't quite sick of him yet. I'm actually never sick of him.

It's a light conversation for most of the way, until I move my hair behind my ear and the glove hugging my left arm slips a little. He sees. I guiltily dodge his eyes and try to keep walking like nothing happened, but he puts a firm hand on my shoulder.

"Hold on a minute," he says.

I struggle to get out of his grip before he pulls the gloves from my left and then right arms until they're just each dangling loosely from one of his hands. Then he looks on me with true abhorrence.

The branchy gashes from wrist to forearm are a stomach-clenching mix of recently-torn flesh-pink and stitch-black. My arm practically looks borrowed from Frankenstein's monster. His expression seems to contain so many things—disappointment, revulsion, pain....I've shattered his entire image of who I am.

But then his face changes to that usual softness that I'm so accustomed to.

"Oh, Kalana," he says. "I had no idea you were so sad."

He pulls me into his arms, and I cry harder than I ever have, because again he's excused me when I don't deserve it.

There's no excuse for this. None. How can he still like me when he sees? I don't deserve him.

"It's okay, Kalana," he whispers into my ear as I sob. "It's okay. Just promise me you'll get some help. And the next time you feel that awful come to me. I won't let you hurt yourself."

If only it were that simple. But I nod so he'll stop saying such impossibly wonderful things.

I cry for a long time. When the tears finally cease, I can't help asking "Why do you still like me?" weakly into his ear.

When he pulls back, he looks me square in the face. Then says something I don't expect.

"Because you're wonderful," he says as if it's the most natural truth in the world.

If I wasn't already tapped out, it would be enough to make me burst into tears all over again, but my tear ducts feel physically unable to produce anything more.

He sees me to my door, and before he leaves asks, "Do you want me to talk to your father with you?"

"He already knows," I say. He can tell from my shamed expression that it's true. "We're working on it."

If only we were working on it and actually getting somewhere.

"Well, good," he says before planting a shy kiss on my cheek.

"Stay in touch, you," he adds, with a playful pinch of my chin. Then he's gone. And I wish like hell he wasn't.

At lunch the next day, my thoughts are so wrapped around Tobias, I don't realize I'm subconsciously staring right at someone I barely know, Eddie Sherman.

When our eyes connect, he looks away so quickly it catches my attention. Then he leaves the lunch room suddenly, even though he's left a full, untouched lunch tray at his table.

Startled by this strange reaction, I follow him to the courtyard, where he's sitting with his back to me on a short wall of stone.

When I come up behind him and tap his shoulder, his whole body jerks.

"Eddie, is something wrong?" I ask.

"No, no," he insists. But he seems fidgety. Yet I can't imagine what this could be about.

"You know if you ever need to talk to someone..."

"You?" he asks, like the idea is ridiculous.

I guess a lot of people in school have guessed I'm a cutter by now, so that does sound like a slightly nut-bar solution, but I'm still hurt.

"*Yeah,*" I snap. "Just because I'm the sheriff's daughter doesn't mean I'm the enemy."

He just stares at me blankly, like I'm the one acting strangely.

"Did you see something the other night? When Tommy was killed?" I ask him. "At school?"

"I didn't see anything. Nothing," he insists before he grabs his backpack and bolts.

This is weird.

I relay everything to my dad that evening, and he listens with a tight and tame expression. I wonder if he's even hearing me.

"So what are you gonna do about Eddie?" I ask.

"Nothing," my dad huffs. "If Eddie Sherman has anything

to say, he'll come to me himself."

"But he's terrified of something. I can tell he wants to talk, but he's scared to death. He probably saw the murder. He probably knows who did it."

"That's a lot of assumptions, Kalana," my dad says. Then he dares to dismiss me with, "He probably just has a crush on you or something."

I glower at him.

"Of course, because anything that happens within high school walls must have something to do with hormones. Jesus, Dad!" I snap.

"Don't take the son of God's name in vain," he says.

"Imagine if you could hear everyone, all the time and people just went around saying your name all day when they weren't even talking to you. Can you appreciate how irritating that would be?"

I roll my eyes. He always says this if I happen to let a "Jesus" or, God forbid, a "God" slip in total frustration. It was cute the first time, but now it just sounds crazy. Does he really believe that?

"But, Dad, I'm worried about Eddie. He was really scared. What if he's next just because he saw?"

"He's not," my dad insists. "He's a good kid."

But that answer doesn't remotely satisfy me and it partially scares me. The way my dad said that makes me think he has some kind of insight into the mind of the person doing these things. Like he knows who it is. Like he's supporting this vigilante.

But surely my dad isn't capable of aiding a murderer. I mean, yeah, he cared about Billy too. We had him and Tobias over for dinner three times a week back in those days. But he wouldn't stand by and let someone kill children, no matter how much they deserved it. *Would* he?

But it does bother me the more I think about it. He's been trying to lock them up for a year, and it hasn't been working. And I guess I do kind of get it.

I certainly feel more for the childlike, defenseless Billy, who got beaten to death when he just wanted to play with his toy cars, than those voids of humanity Rodney and Travis—the only two of the five involved in the murder who haven't turned up dead or missing.

The next day, when I sit down next to Morgan in English, she asks why I'm doing my overly-warm knit gloves two days in a row. When they appear, they tend to last until my scars heal, which takes months, so the other kids know better than to ask.

"I'm starting a new trend," I lie with a shrug. It's pretty rehearsed, so it sounds convincing. She doesn't give it a second thought, but some others stare before they see me glaring back and snap their eyes away.

Maybe that's really why they're afraid of me. I wouldn't want to hang with a cutter either.

Blackout

Aside from the sleepwalking, I occasionally blackout, like I did the night my mom was killed, but it's only happened one other time.

I was walking home late one night after a chemistry lab and heard a woman scream. Instead of running away from the sound, for some bizarre reason, I ran toward it. In the darkness of the large playground in the middle of the town, I saw outlines of a struggle between a large man and a small woman with her young son watching, stiff with fear. And then, blackness. I woke up at the playground covered in blood, alone.

I went home, and my dad was terrified. He asked if the blood was mine, and I said I didn't know. I had somehow managed to slash my wrists that time too, so *probably*, but there seemed to be more of it than usual, and even though I required a transfusion that day (luckily my father and I are both type O), I didn't need as much blood as the gallons spattered on my clothes seemed to suggest.

No one ever reported any crime that night or saw anything, so we just kind of moved on. But my dad was more concerned about this blackout than the sleepwalking, and he still asks me sporadically if it's ever happened again.

It hasn't, but lately I'm starting to wonder about this second incident in my repertoire that's odd, involves slashed wrists and doesn't really seem to involve sleepwalking.

It's especially strange when I walk home from school really late after another extra-credit chemistry lab. (I'm hopelessly behind.)

Soon, I see the little boy from the incident on that same playground standing and staring at me. His eyes are that creepy blue that always startles me, and he seems in awe of me. It's the same way that—

Nurse Roberts takes his hand, and her similar eyes lock on me. The boy from that night is her son?

She seems dumbstruck—they both do, actually—so I speak first.

"Hello, Mrs. Roberts," I say cordially. "I didn't know you had a son."

Both their faces drop at this statement.

"You *didn't*?" the little boy asks, suddenly not as startled by me. Instead his tone seems to ask me, "Are you a moron?"

Maybe he's been in the office visiting his mom one of the many times I've been there, but I don't remember seeing him. I feel insensitive.

"No," I squeak guiltily. Man, I am just a horrible person. How unobservant and selfish can I be?

The little boy turns to his mom. "Mom, is she—?"

"She doesn't remember, sweetie," his mom cuts him off, not taking her eyes from mine. "It was a long time ago."

The little boy doesn't seem satisfied by this.

"Well, I *do* remember seeing you," I say to the boy, "but...that was *you* that night?" I ask Mrs. Roberts. "Who screamed?"

She doesn't answer. She just stares. Her stare is so creepy I decide the best course of action is to walk away. Obviously this woman isn't right in the head.

"Well, goodnight," I say before I attempt to walk past them. But her words stop me.

"I know some people think you're a demon," Mrs. Roberts says. "But I think you're an angel of God."

What?

I'm so terrified by her further creepiness that I walk home a little faster.

I can't help but tell Morgan about this strange incident, without explaining the even weirder one that came before it, during English the next day. But she doesn't seem as creeped out by Nurse Roberts and her grandiose compliment.

"Isn't it kind of normal for older women to call younger girls angels, especially nurses?" Morgan asks.

"I guess, but she's always staring at me in this weird way when she's giving me transfusions."

"Transfusions?" Morgan jumps on my revealing mistake a little faster than I would've guessed.

"I mean, taking blood," I save quickly. But her eyes instantly go to the thick gloves still hiding the gashes on my wrists.

"Why are you still wearing those gloves?" she asks me again, almost curtly.

"It's too hot for sleeves," I explain, which is true. I'd much rather wear long sleeves right now, but that wouldn't look like a fashion statement. It would just look weirdly off-season in September in Texas, which still feels like summer.

"So why are you *wearing gloves*?" she asks, easily exposing the hole in my false logic.

I have no answer for that, so for the rest of English, I just say nothing.

But I need someone to talk to, so I end up telling her everything during PE after we sneak out and sit in the field behind the gym again.

Needless to say, she's a little startled.

"So you sleepwalk, have blackouts and slash your own wrists?" she sums it all up, I think, just to process it.

"Two blackouts," I correct her.

"Where you saved a little boy and his mother," she says.

"*Saved?*"

"There was obviously a man attacking her. And now she's calling you an angel of God. Don't you think you must've done something for her?"

"The man I remember seeing was huge. I'm tiny. There's no way I saved her. I probably just scared him away by being there."

"And then you cut your own wrists and passed out."

"Apparently."

"Why would you want to hurt yourself?"

"I have no idea."

Now she's staring at my off-season gloves, probably imagining what's underneath, but she's too polite to ask.

"You wanna see?" I ask with a sigh, knowing what the answer will be.

She slowly and intensely nods. I glance around us. Except for a few guys playing soccer in the field behind us, Tobias included, there's no one close by.

I slide off one glove and watch her expression twist to total horror at the sight of the branchy, thick and stomach-turning gash that makes a messy, unclean cut from wrist to forearm. The stitches make it even worse. They're black against the torn, pinkish skin.

"Gross," she breathes with a slow release, like she's thinking the word "cool" in her head but is too nice to actually say it.

Then she just stares until I replace the glove to break her trance.

"I think there's some stuff I need to tell you," she says, surprising me. I can't imagine anything she'd need to share with me. She seems very what-you-see-is-what-you-get. But I restrain myself so I won't laugh in her face. "I've heard some really weird rumors about you."

My face falls. Rumors? *Plural?* I thought the very probable rumor about the cutting was bad enough.

It turns out to be stupid high school stuff that no one would believe, but it's still strange that these rumors revolve around me.

Apparently, I'm in a cult and a bloodletter who cuts herself because she aspires to be a vampire, and I've slept with every guy involved in Billy Engel's death, Tommy even after his death and Billy and Tobias at the same time. (Really? Travis must've started that one. It's especially ridiculous because I've never even been on a real date or even kissed anyone.) But those are the lighter rumors. The most hurtful one is that I had a rage blackout and killed my mother and then had a rage blackout and killed Billy a year later. It just makes me sick. Kids are so cruel.

When she's done nervously explaining all this crap to me as gently as she can, all I can say is, "How do you aspire to be a vampire?"

"Yeah, it's all pretty weird."

"Except the cutting part," I admit. "They got that right."

"But you have no memory of it. You're a sleepwalker."

"Who occasionally blacks out."

"Who blacked out *twice*."

"And scared away a giant man. Then woke up covered in blood."

Morgan's face seems to catch on that last statement. Then she asks me, "Did they ever test the blood that was all over you?"

"Yes," I say easily. But the next words catch in my throat.

"Nurse Roberts did," I realize. "She said it was all mine."

Morgan poses the question I'm already struggling with. "What if she lied?"

Why would she do that? To protect me? From what?

I have to talk to Mrs. Roberts again. I cut my last class to hit the emergency center, knowing Mrs. Roberts is most likely still working. I expect her to be annoyed when she sees me, but she isn't.

She's still looking at me with that worshipping stare, and I really want to know why, but over the counter of the emergency clinic isn't the right setting.

"Can you take a break?" I ask her.

She nods and follows me outside.

"What happened that night?" I ask when we're alone.

"Child, I think you should just leave it," she says simply.

"But you were being attacked..."

"I was."

"And I...*saved* you?"

"Yes, and your daddy will kill me if I tell you how."

"My dad?"

"He's the one you should ask about this. I suspect it's a family thing," she absolutely stuns me by saying. "But I will be forever thankful for what you did for me and my boy. And I will never breathe a word of it to anyone. I *swear*."

Then she returns inside, and I'm left standing outside, reminding myself to breathe.

It's hard to bring this up to Dad at dinner, especially over his happy grunts due to the deliciousness of his own food, so I just dive right in. This has all gotten too weird to leave alone.

"Did you know that I saved Mrs. Roberts and her son the night I blacked out?" I ask.

I expect him to drop his fork, but he doesn't. His expression is guarded but not surprised.

"What do you mean, *saved*?" he asks, the same way I first said that word, like it's completely implausible.

"I don't know. She won't tell me," I admit. "But she said I saved her from a large man, and she called me an angel of God." I probably should've left out that last part. It makes her sound crazy.

"That woman strikes me as a little odd," he says gently. "I wouldn't put much stock in anything she says."

"But I remember seeing her and her son being attacked by someone before I blacked out."

"I remember you seeing someone get attacked, but I didn't know it was Mrs. Roberts."

"I didn't either until I ran into her and her son the other day," I say, not mentioning shanghaiing her at work today. "I recognized *him*."

"Oh, I see." He thinks a long while, and it makes me nervous, but when he talks, it's dismissive. "I imagine you cut your wrists and passed out. That would scare someone away, maybe even a psycho. She's probably too polite to talk about the specifics."

I guess it kind of makes sense. But the way she was talking was like I was some kind of superhero. But what kind of lame super power is wrist-slashing? But I guess it is the most plausible.

"I don't want to hurt myself anymore," I say heavily. He just stares at me, waiting to see where this is headed. "I want to see a therapist."

He's not thrilled about the idea. I can tell. Waste of money and time. It got mom nowhere. But he can tell I'm serious about this and won't back down until I get my way.

"Are you sure that's what you really want?" he asks.

"I'm sorry about the money—"

"It's not the money. I'm worried about *you*. You might not like what you find."

"What does *that* mean?"

"Maybe there's a reason your brain is protecting you from

whatever happened those nights."

"Well, wouldn't you want to know what that is?" *I* want to know.

"I'm not so sure," he says, before rinsing his plate in the sink and placing it in the dishwasher. "You know what they say. Never wake a sleepwalker."

Then he disappears upstairs without another word.

Psychology 101

My first session with Mrs. Lane is weird. She's *weird*.

She's really intrusive, and she asks all these highly personal questions. She doesn't really seem to be getting to the issue at hand *at all*—the cutting, the blackouts, the sleepwalking....

She's more concerned with my relationship with my mother and father, and if they've ever touched me in places covered by a bathing suit. The answer's no. She goes so far with similar questions that I have to stop her.

"Why are we talking about sexual abuse? I've never been sexually abused by anyone," I tell her.

"Many people with repressed memories have been sexually abused at some point in their lives. It's how they learn to cope with unwanted memories."

"No one has touched me in any naughty places, *ever*," I over-clarify with annoyance.

"Well, how can you be sure? I suspect you're seeing something so awful that you're repressing it, which makes sexual abuse likely."

"Well, do repressed memories always involve sexual abuse, or is it sometimes something else?"

"They can also result from witnessing or being the

recipient of violence or some similar traumatic event."

That sounds a little more like it. "From what I remember from the two times I blacked out, violence is more likely."

"Well, that would have to be *some* violence," Mrs. Lane says with an insensitive laugh. "With TV these days. Your generation is so desensitized."

I'm starting to suspect that Mrs. Lane is a really crappy therapist, but at least she's gotten my thinking this far. "Well, I woke up covered in blood one of those times."

"Yes, you mentioned. From slashed wrists."

"I think it was too much blood to be just from my wrists."

"But you did have a transfusion that day, yes?"

This stumps me.

"I think the real question we need to ask, Kalana, is, 'Why do you want to kill yourself?'"

I'm stunned into silence and feel my cheeks flush. I hate her for thinking that this is a question I need to answer. "Well, I don't," I spit angrily. "That's why this is so confusing."

"Well, part of you wants to die or you wouldn't keep trying."

So this is what my dad was trying to protect me from. Quacks running wild with ridiculously incorrect assumptions.

Maybe he's right. Maybe I am just a sleepwalker, with two isolated incidents of blacking-out. And maybe I blacked out, cut my wrists and terrified a robber away. And Nurse Roberts didn't fake the blood results. Maybe it really is that simple. What is it we learn in science? The simplest explanation is usually the right one? I'm starting to think therapy is a waste of money.

"Kalana," Mrs. Lane says my name like she's chewing it. "Have you ever wondered how you cut yourself every time?"

"Well, *yes*, that's why I'm here." I snap. I seriously have 45 more minutes of this? If I leave early, do a get a discount?

"No, I mean physically how? Where does the sharp object come from? Do you ever find any kitchen knives with blood on them or any sharp rocks?"

"No," I admit, downcast. "We've never been able to figure that out."

"That's very curious," Mrs. Lane says before writing more notes on her pad and then saying nothing for what seems like too long a time, like she's purposely waiting out the clock too.

That's it? You're just going to pose a question and not answer it? "So what do you think that means?" I push, knowing she probably doesn't know or she'd say. But I need to get something out of this overpriced session.

"I'm not sure at this time," she says in an airy, annoyingly coy voice.

Ugh.

We sit there for several long moments, neither saying a thing. Soon I'm staring her in the eye just to see if she'll stare back. She's not comfortable holding my gaze and often looks away to eye the clock. Wuss.

"So that's it?" I ask when it seems like we're not going to talk anymore. We still have 40 minutes left.

"That's up to you. Do you have anything else to share?"

"I've told you everything I know," I say, and it's true, which is unfortunate because it seems she's hit a wall.

"I know," she says. "And that's the problem. I think you know more. We have to unlock those memories."

"How?"

"Have you ever tried hypnosis?"

I roll my eyes inadvertently, and she takes that as my answer.

"I'm surprised you've decided to see a therapist if you don't believe in therapy."

"I don't know," I snap defensively. "I just thought you'd be more helpful or have...*answers* or something."

"We can find them together, but only if you work *with* me," she claims.

I'm really not sure about any of this.

"Well, since we have *38 minutes* left, I guess we can try hypnosis, but it may not work on me," I warn her.

We try. She has me lay on the couch I've been sitting on (how cliché) and imagine I'm on a beach, listening to the waves rushing in and out. She's speaking in this airy voice describing the beach to me and simulating the waves with her voice. "You're lying on a beach...listening to the waves rushing in and out...your body is completely relaxed...you feel weightless...." It's hilarious, and I'm fighting hard not to laugh.

But I give it a real try. And there's this moment when I'm so relaxed and comfortable that I feel like I might drift to sleep, which would be a much better way to spend the remainder of the session. Then the light behind my eyes dims. The light generated by this well-lit office is shrinking to a pinpoint, like I'm standing at the end of a long, circling dark tunnel.

I guess I'm falling asleep very slowly, but I've never seen this visual before. Then a very noisy wind-up alarm sounds, and I'm jerked back to full consciousness.

"Well, that's the end of the session," Mrs. Lane says and

removes herself from the room without another look or word.

Okay...So I'll just let myself out.

In the car, my dad asks how it went. I tell him he might be right about therapy in general, and he can't help letting out a self-satisfied huff.

"But I'll give it a real go before I give up," I say, surprising us both.

I can't help wondering about that black tunnel. Was that just a hyper-aware loss of consciousness or something else? If we hadn't run out of time, would she have succeeded in hypnotizing me?

I tell Morgan about the therapy session behind the gym during PE (today we're doing indoor soccer...or something).

And she tells me these really scary stories about male therapists hypnotizing their female patients and molesting them.

"Ewww. What is it with everyone and molestation lately?" I snap at her. It's literally the last thing I'd ever want to talk about.

She guiltily changes the subject. "Do you think all this has to do with your mother's death?" Morgan asks the question I'm surprised my therapist didn't.

"I wasn't home when it happened," I tell Morgan with a

shrug. "It was just a drive-by." *Probably*. My dad's not convinced.

"What does your dad think?"

I take a minute before I answer this question. I've never told anyone this before, but it's nice to have someone to talk to about it.

"He thinks Travis's father ordered it and made it look like drug dealers."

"What? Why?"

As Morgan also knows, Travis's father is the owner of the Haven Hotel, and he's always done well, despite the fact that Haven isn't really big on tourism.

"He says there's no tourism in this town and the drug dealers were the only ones to ever buy rooms at his hotel, so they could do their deals."

"That seems kind of..."

"Thin? Yeah. But he's still looking for proof."

At my second weekly therapy session, we get right to the hypnosis so we don't run out of time.

It takes 30 minutes for the tunnel shrinking away from the light pinpoint to appear. Then it goes completely black, and I slide into this weird space between asleep and awake. I can tell I'm neither, because I feel completely detached from Mrs. Lane's voice. I can hear it, but it sounds distant and muffled. But she's still going on in her silly, airy voice about waves rushing in and out around me and how I'm weightless.

She's so fucking stupid! This isn't hypnotism! She's just boring me to sleep! Nothing is happening!

Then I feel really hot, like my skin is about to melt off, I have a splitting headache, my stomach hurts, and I feel like I'm about to scream or throw up to release all the pain and nausea.

But I don't scream. Instead I feel this unexpected release. It's wonderful. Then a blacker blackness engulfs me, and I slip into total void.

When I open my eyes, my chin is pinned to my chest, and I see my wrists covered in blood. The stitches are cut. There's blood all over my lap and some splattered on her white couch.

I look over to where Mrs. Lane sits in her pink armchair, and she has one hand clasped over her mouth with a dead look in her wet eyes.

"What happened?" I ask her, sitting up and trickling blood onto my lap.

She doesn't answer me or even glance in my direction. I'm not even sure she hears me.

"Mrs. Lane?"

Nothing. It's like she's gone catatonic.

"Mrs. Lane! What happened?"

It's like we're in different rooms. She's not even acknowledging my presence.

"Did you see me cut myself? Did you see where I got the knife?"

"I didn't mean to set you off," Mrs. Lane finally answers me in a weak voice, still not meeting my eyes, even when I try and crouch to meet her gaze. She just moves her eyes.

"So you saw?"

Finally, her heavy eyes find mine, and she holds them for a short moment.

Then she just says, "I can't help you," as firmly as she can, though her voice wavers.

Then she leaves the room in a daze, groping her way out like a blind person. Like she doesn't know where she's going or even where she is.

That's pretty much my last session with Mrs. Lane.

When I approach the car, my father's eyes fall on me, and his whole body jerks in reaction to the blood. Then he just bows his head and shakes it slowly. When I climb in, he can't keep himself from saying, "I told you therapy wasn't a good idea." But I just stare out the window as we move toward the emergency center, neither acknowledging nor denying his statement. The rest of the ride is wordless.

Even Dr. Menzer doesn't say much as he stitches me up that day, which isn't completely unheard of. But he usually makes a couple of insensitive jokes about how I need to stop falling on these knives, especially since he just fixed me. But not today. I also have a different nurse, a new one who's more than a little alarmed by my predicament.

Predicament. I can't stop mind-chewing that word as Morgan prattles on about the upcoming homecoming dance. It's lunchtime, and we're eating alone at a table, like usual.

Is this really just the way I am? Is there really nothing I can do? I've seen a therapist and often a doctor who gives me enough medication to sink a rhinoceros, yet here I am, still having this odd problem that doesn't make sense.

And what did Mrs. Lane see? I guess seeing me get a hold of something sharp in her office and cut myself must've been traumatic, but why would a therapist have a sharp object in her office? And where did it go?

And it's strange what she said: "I didn't mean to set you off." Those words were picked so deliberately, like they mean something more than just the cutting.

Set me off. What sets me off besides falling asleep?

"Kalana?" Morgan rips through my thoughts. "Are you listening?"

I want to tell her to shut her face. I'm mulling over actual problems and not stupid high school shit.

"Yes. Something about a *dance*?" I snap, curtly. Her expression is wounded though, and then I feel bad. She's just making conversation, and I'm getting snippy with her about it.

My tone completely changes. "I'm sorry I just... have stuff on my mind."

Morgan nods, not even needing to ask what that is. "I just thought you might want to think about something else for a change," she says. "Something fun. Like a dance." And she really means the word "fun" when she describes "dance." She's so naive.

Dances at Haven High aren't fun. Travis usually heckles everyone who walks by his little huddle of sociopaths (though that huddle has gotten a little smaller these days) and, by the end of the night, attacks at least one girl with unwanted advances. And he's eyeing Morgan right now. He tends to stare at her during lunch, regularly. I'm not surprised she gains admirers so easily, but Travis isn't an admirer you want.

He just flicked a paper football at the back of her head. When she looks back to see who sent it, her smile falls, and she's truly disturbed by the source of the attention.

I glare back at him.

"Ignore him," I tell her, tapping her shoulder so she'll turn back to me. "If you want to go to the dance so badly, I'll go with you," I tell her then silently add to myself, "to protect you from Travis."

Not that Travis has ever been particularly afraid of my father.

I actually kind of hope he does something bad enough for my father to be able to take action against him, but I doubt it. He'll probably just toe the line so perfectly that no one can prosecute.

Ugh. This dance is going to suck.

That weekend, we get ready together. I've purposely missed the last few Haven dances so I do have a rush of excitement getting ready despite my best efforts to resist such feelings.

But I am a little embarrassed by the white kidskin gloves I wear with my red halter dress to hide my newly reopened gashes. If

I bleed, it's going to show up way too easily, but mostly I'm upset because it looks like I'm trying to pull off some kinky Jessica Rabbit impersonation. Thankfully I don't have red hair, or it would be really over the top.

"Maybe I shouldn't have picked red," I say with regret into the small mirror above my vanity table as I pull on the second glove.

"You look great!" Morgan claims before she knocks me from the mirror to apply mascara for the 10th time.

Morgan has a complicated updo, spiked silver heels and an icy blue dress that perfectly matches her eyes. The bodice is even made up of some intricate white beading, which means it easily cost $300 plus.

It puts the halter dress I found at a vintage shop to shame. But it does go well with the red velvet platforms I'm wearing—also vintage. They were Mom's.

But I display the angel necklace Billy gave me proudly. I've never let anyone see it, but tonight feels like the right time for some reason.

"No, *you* look great," I object, watching her shake with such nervous excitement she has difficulty coating the lashes of her second eye. If only the dance wasn't going to be such a let-down for her. But maybe it won't be. She seems to find enjoyment in just about anything.

It's then that my doorbell strangely rings, but I can't imagine who would show up right now. But when I hear my dad answer the door, I recognize that tone in his voice. It's the sound of overwhelming approval. I know who it is before Morgan and I descend the stairs. I will myself not to turn as red as my dress.

"Kalana," Dad says excitedly when Morgan and I enter the living room.

"Look who's here to pick you up! It's Tobias," he tells me, like I can't see Tobias standing right next to him, dressed casually in jeans, a white shirt and a black sportcoat.

He looks undeniably nice. I muster the biggest smile I can but feel it filtered by shyness. Not that Tobias cares. He smiles as freely as he would if his brother were still alive.

"You look beautiful, Kalana," he tells me after a fairly obvious once-over, then notices Morgan beaming next to me and adds that we "both look very pretty." It's sweet of him to try and lump me in with Morgan. Like I could ever look pretty next to her.

"So what are you doing here?" I can't keep myself from asking, while trying very hard not to sound ungrateful for his presence.

"I thought I'd escort you ladies to the dance," he says, his elbows stuck out on either side. Morgan easily takes the closest free arm with a laugh.

"Well, of course, kind sir," she says in her best Southern Belle impersonation. It's so damn cute. I want to throw things at her head.

"Kalana?" Tobias asks hopefully, pointing his free elbow at me.

"Why didn't you tell me you wanted to go with us?" I ask.

"I was afraid you'd hide in your room," he gleans accurately. I can't deny that might've happened if I'd known his plan.

My jaw clenches as I take his free elbow, but I try very hard to smile despite it.

When we enter the gym, Morgan says it looks like "fairy land," while I just see a bunch of twinkle lights strung around the ceiling and walls. I also notice way too many dark corners for Travis to grope people in. I guess I'm a pessimist.

But I only feel that way until I see Travis's pervy eyes following Morgan wherever she walks; Tobias sees it too. Then I realize I'm just a realist. I stay close to Morgan as she bounces around, excited about all the cheap paper-rolled decorations, and

Tobias stays close to me.

"You know, I only came because Morgan wanted to," I tell him. "If I had known you wanted to go...I mean, you two could've gone together."

"Well, I only came because you were coming," he tells me, without a hint of hesitation in his voice.

I don't know how he manages being so raw and honest. I'd be too embarrassed. But then he tops his level of honesty even more.

"And I would've asked if you and I could just go together, alone. Like a date," he clarifies so well that I can no longer pretend to misunderstand his intentions. "But I didn't want to leave your friend Morgan out."

Speaking of Morgan, she's found the punch, and she's examining each individual plastic teacup like they're something special. We both can't help cracking up.

"I mean, look how much fun she's having," Tobias says.

But then, unfortunately, Travis apprehends Morgan right when she's excitedly tasting her cup of sherbet and soda.

"Your ass looks hot in that dress," Travis tells Morgan right when Tobias and I arrive.

Gee. How can she not swoon after that?

She's instantly uncomfortable and pretends she doesn't hear him, tucking her hair behind her ear and eyeing her silver heels.

"Back off, Travis," Tobias says while sliding between them, meeting his eyes straight on. There's a latent anger there that I don't expect from Tobias despite who he's talking to. It's unnerving.

Despite facing the boy whose brother he cruelly murdered, Travis somehow has the audacity to look me up and down and give me an ear-to-ear smile.

"You don't look so bad either," he tells me.

Tobias takes a step forward until his searing eyes are inches from the ones who took someone so important away from him.

"What's up, Engel? You've got something to say?"

But I don't want Tobias to get hurt or become something he's not by hurting someone else, even if that person deserves it.

I gently take his hand and lightly tug it. He feels my touch, and the vengeful anger cools in his eyes a little as he takes a step away.

"That's what I thought," Travis gloats before he slinks away.

Once he's gone, Morgan asks me, "What's his problem?"

"He thinks charming and date rape are the same thing," I explain. Then I very seriously add, "Stay away from dark corners."

I try to stay with Morgan all night, but I get exhausted by her enthusiasm, and it isn't long before Eddie catches my eye.

He's actually staring at my kidskin gloves deep in thought, and he's startled when he realizes I'm looking back at him. Tobias follows me in confusion as I cut Eddie off before he can duck into the hallway.

"How's your chemistry grade?" I pretend to make small talk with a transparent smile. I suspect Eddie actually dropped the chemistry class we had together so he could avoid me. I haven't seen him in weeks.

"It's great," he says awkwardly, knowing he's caught.

Then he notices Tobias and leans in closer in the hope that only he and I can hear, which is unsuccessful.

"You don't need to harass me, you know," he says. "You have nothing to fear."

Fear? "What do you mean?"

"I would never tell," he says, like what he just said actually made sense. "Just like I told your dad when he came asking."

"*What?*"

At this, he gives me a flabbergasted look I don't understand. I look to Tobias, and it's clear that he hasn't the faintest clue what we're talking about in general.

I'm about to ask what hell he means when the horns of the live swing band screech through our conversation. It's so unbelievably loud. And that's when I look around and realize I have no idea where Morgan is.

I check all the poorly lit areas of the gym until I find myself behind the stage itself—the area behind the part of the room generating the most noise. And it's then that I hear Morgan's soft cries. "Please...stop," she sobs. I run toward the source of the crying and only half-realize that both Eddie and Tobias are following close on my heels.

It isn't long before we find them: Robert and Travis with Morgan between them, forced on her hands and knees.

Robert is holding Morgan's arms and Travis is hiking up her dress, tearing down her panties and putting her into position. They're both exposed. Travis is about to....

Then time stops. The tunnel swirls around my vision, until the pinpoint of light is created and then slips away completely.

Then I get really hot, nauseated, and I feel like I'm about to scream and throw-up with *Exorcist* intensity.

But I don't. Instead I float out of my own body and see my face frozen into a twisted expression of rage I've never seen on my own face. And that's not all. My eyes are fully black, which is beyond creepy.

This must be that strange detachment thing Mrs. Lane was talking about. I'm not really seeing what's happening. I'm seeing what I think is happening when I'm really still inside my body, denying what I'm seeing.

Is Morgan getting raped right now while I've completely shut down to repress this memory? But it doesn't feel true. I don't hear her crying anymore. I don't hear anything, in fact, except the faint murmurs of the horns like they're echoing in some far away chasm.

I float further to examine the frozen faces of everyone around me—Morgan with black tears streaming from her eyes, Tobias truly unsettled, Travis and Robert with their mouths gaping open—all have horrified expressions aimed at me, except Eddie.

He looks completely unsurprised. In fact, he's actually smiling with half his face, which seems really inappropriate. And there's even a hint of guilt in his expression because he knows it's wrong to smile.

What's about to happen that entertains him against his

will?

All I know is that when I saw Travis about to hurt Morgan like that—force something so personal and unwelcome. I. GOT. SO. ANGRY. He's evil. He help beat Billy Engel to death too.

He deserves to—

Everything goes black. The void strikes. But just before that I hear a completely inhuman voice slur the word "Muuuuurddddeeeerrrers."

The voice is mine.

Afterblood

When I wake, I can feel the hard sectioned wood floor of the gym against my bare back, and I'm not surprised to see the kidskin gloves shredded and barely clinging to my wrists, which are caked in blood.

So are my legs and, I suspect, my dress, but I can't tell because of its dark red color.

Morgan, Eddie and Tobias stand over me. Morgan looks completely terrified. Eddie looks expectant. Tobias has a completely impassive expression as he helps me up.

I step toward Morgan to see if she's alright, but she shrinks away oddly. Travis and Robert are nowhere in sight, and it's like the area behind the stage was decorated by Jackson Pollock gone psycho. There's blood everywhere, and it's not mine, I deduce, since there's a pile of shredded human and tuxedo at my feet. I did this. I'm in shock. But I can't help but notice that it's only enough flesh for one person. It is Rodney or Travis? But I spot the white Chrysanthemum, blood-spattered but still in one piece, that had been pinned to Rodney's lapel.

"What did I do?" I ask Morgan.

She doesn't answer. She has that same catatonic look as Mrs. Lane. She just stares at the mound that used to be a person,

77

no longer crying.

"You mean she doesn't know?" Eddie asks Morgan. She slowly turns and faces him with a blank expression but doesn't answer him either.

"So you really don't remember what happens to you when...this happens?" he asks me.

Could you be more vague?

"No. What happens?! That's what I've been asking you!" I yell, really losing my cool now, not that anyone can hear anything over those swing horns. "Why won't you tell me?"

Eddie jumps back from me like he thinks I'll hurt him. I would never. Would I?

Tobias takes an unafraid step toward me and holds up the mess that is currently my left arm.

"Kalana, you're really bleeding," he says, putting whatever just happened aside like it isn't a concern. "You need to see a doctor."

How can he say that after what I just did and whatever he just witnessed? What is wrong with everyone?

"No! I need someone to finally tell me what the hell is going on! What happened?"

Eddie just grimaces at me unsurely so I turn to Morgan.

She recoils from me like I could stab her with my desperate stare. She's afraid of me?

Tobias continues examining my cut-up arms with concern. I don't understand. Is he in shock?

"Morgan, she won't hurt you," Eddie says for me, which I really appreciate, until he feels the need to follow it up with, "I don't *think*...."

I sneer at him. *Thanks, Eddie.*

"Of course, she wouldn't," Tobias snaps at Eddie. "She just saved her."

"Morgan, I would never," I say, sounding way more sure of myself than I currently feel.

"Morgan," Tobias says her name suddenly to grab her attention back. She's in such shock it's like we have to say her name just to snap her back to reality.

"Take my car and take Kalana to the hospital," he tells her gently, dangling his car keys in her face.

Morgan takes the keys but seems barely able to see straight, let alone drive, so I snatch them from her.

"Why don't you go with me?" I ask Tobias, thinking that he's the most coherent and could possibly explain things. He's also the only person I'm comfortable being alone with right now. I could never hurt Tobias. *Right*?

"We're going to clean up this mess," he says to Eddie's dismay, gesturing to both of them.

Clean up? "Is that a good idea? My father needs to—"

"I'm not letting anyone hurt you for saving Morgan from being raped by the same two guys who murdered my brother," Tobias says heavily. I guess I can't blame him for that point of view.

"Kalana. *Go*," Tobias orders me in a commanding voice I've never heard from him before. "You're going to bleed out."

Then he and Eddie head in the direction of the hall and the janitor's closet, and I'm left standing alone. I mean, really alone because it seems Morgan ran off when we weren't focused on her.

Shit. Now there's no one to explain.

I get into Tobias's aged white sedan and sit in the driver's seat thinking before I head toward the emergency center. I've gotten so used to almost bleeding out that I'm probably overly calm in these situations now, when really I could lose consciousness or slip into a coma and die any second.

But I feel fine, and that makes me wonder again where the knives come from and how someone like me—tiny, weak—could possibly tear someone apart.

Then for the first time, even though I've been to the emergency room several times now for slashed wrists, it occurs to me to look inside myself, something I've always been afraid to do in fear that I'll injure myself further, for the source of these elusive knives. But I have to know.

I peel back the pink and painful skin of one wrist, forcing out more blood, until I find something that I've never seen in my anatomy class.

It looks like the bloom of an unripe flower all folded in, but covered in blood, and this collection of instruments packed together like a Swiss Army knife are *bones.*

They're a strange collection of sharp, extra bones inside my small wrist, all clumped together like they're stored there and have the ability to fold out into something much larger.

The bone-knives have five points, and there's even more bone coiling around them like the links of a chain. Like they extend out on chains of bone, fan out and cut things up.

What the hell is this?

I fight my gag reflex and turn the key in the ignition, finally starting to feel woozy from the blood loss.

While Dr. Menzer stitches up my wrists after giving me some of Dad's blood he keeps on hand for this, I think he can already tell this isn't a normal visit, especially when he notices the state of my right wrist, more opened up than the other.

No jokes. No snide remarks. He just waits for me to ask.

"I found the knives," I say coldly, scrutinizing his expression. He doesn't give me much aside from a deep sigh, and then he cuts the stitch off and gets up. Poker must be his game, or he just genuinely doesn't care...seemingly about anything.

Without a response, he goes to a safe in the room and enters a combination, and then he brings out something I've never seen before: X-rays.

He lights up a part of the wall and displays them for two arms side-by-side. There are the strange bone anomalies, identical in each wrist, lit up brightly for me to see clearly.

They're a little easier to see when not bathed in blood, but they're pretty much what I thought they were. I remember when he took the X-rays, though I never saw the result. It was the night my mom was killed. The first time I ever came in with slashed wrists...

Oh god.

"Did I kill my mother?" I blurt out.

He turns to me, startled by the question. "Goodness no," he says, slapping the X-rays off the display. "You're one of the good guys," he catches my eye to assure me but can't stop himself from adding an unsure, "*I think.*" Careful to add a disclaimer, just like Eddie. Then he puts the X-rays back into the safe and activates the digital lock.

How can he be so sure?

"But I just—"

"No," he cuts me off. "I don't need to know. I don't want to know. And I don't know anything except the existence of those bone abnormalities, and only your father, and now *you*, know that I know about those. So I don't know about those either."

"But Dr. Menzer—"

"No. No. No. No. No. No. No. No," he says while not meeting my eyes, like I'm suddenly not even present in his office, before he walks out. And that's it. Except a shouted, "Keep it clean," over his shoulder.

I'm angry at his avoidance, but I guess he's just protecting himself and me. He's the only doctor who's ever worked on my hands, he's known about the bone abnormalities from our first appointment, and he's told no one. But why has he stayed silent?

Better yet. Why has my dad stayed silent?

There's really only one person I can ask about all of this, and it's long past time he started talking.

I walk into our house and slam the front door hard.

My father, who was previously sitting in his armchair reading, peers up at me with aggravation. It's strange to watch his face slip from annoyance to total concern. It's easy to notice the new stitches and the fresh, blood-soaked bandages since I no longer have the kidskin gloves to cover up with.

"What happened?"

"Big bone-knives came out of my arms and shredded one of two guys who were trying to rape Morgan."

"Who?"

"Rodney Chutney. Travis got away."

My dad looks truly disappointed. I feel the same way. I would've liked to get Travis the most, but what's worse is that he's probably ratting me out to his dad right now as a super freak who shredded his friend. That will lead to consequences for both me and my father.

"You remember doing this?"

"No, but I found the knives after. And Dr. Menzer showed me the X-rays."

"Why'd he show you *that*?"

"Don't worry, he told me literally nothing," I say angrily.

"Good man."

I'm starting to feel my rage boiling over.

"Just like you," I spit angrily.

"I was trying to protect you."

"From myself! In case you haven't noticed, I'm kind of *stuck* with myself!"

I'm getting hot and nauseated. That's bad. I fan myself for a minute and then sit down across from him, waiting, trying to calm down. Trying to take deep breaths.

"Don't worry, you won't hurt me," he assures me. But I'm not so sure.

"Why do I have knives in my arms?"

"I don't know. You were born with them."

"So you knew before mom died, but that was the first time they came out."

"Yes."

"So I was there the night she died or I wouldn't have been...set off," I say, remembering the words Mrs. Lane chose to describe what happened in her office.

"Most likely," my dad says.

"When I saw those in your baby X-rays, I hoped they were just bone abnormalities. That they'd never come out. But deep down I knew they must've had a purpose."

"I want them removed."

"We tried that the first time they came out. They slowly grew back."

That's startling. "What am I?"

"You're my daughter."

"Do *you* have knives?" I ask, gesturing at his wrists, where I've never noticed broken skin.

"No. No knives," he says. "But you certainly got your rage blackouts from me."

The story about my father nearly beating two robbers twice his size half to death makes a lot more sense now.

"And the sleepwalking from my mom."

"Yes."

"But I'm the only one in the family who blacks out, sleepwalks and kills people."

"Not people. Four *murderers* who beat a mentally handicapped boy to death. A friend of yours. That makes you a good guy in my book. And apparently others agree," he claims. "I'm not the only one who's covered for you. Only one of the bodies you've created has ever turned up, and I only disposed of one of them myself."

Tobias and Eddie are cleaning up Rodney right now, while my entire high school dances around them with no idea of the horror scene hidden behind the stage.

I imagine them mopping gallons of blood so that the mop water becomes blood itself and they have to dispose of it too. Carrying mounds of slippery shredded human to the nearest dumpster and lighting it on fire. Washing blood off their hands, stripping to their boxers and burning their clothes.

Tobias will never look at me again after this, and I don't blame him.

And Nurse Roberts must've done the same thing. The man in the dark that night must've been Preston Owen, one of the five murderers who was thought to have fled to Mexico just like Blaine Spencer. But after what my dad just said, I suspect Blaine never fled to Mexico either. As he just said. He's disposed of one body himself. It must've been Blaine.

And Mrs. Roberts somehow managed to wipe the remains of Preston Owen out of existence. Even my dad didn't find any evidence of a death that night, when he was looking pretty hard so he could dispose of any evidence himself. Just like he disposed of Blaine to protect me. Dad. Mrs. Roberts. Tobias and Eddie. They're all protecting me, but do I deserve it?

"So that's why two of the five killers have mysteriously all fled to Mexico," I say. "And why you haven't tried very hard to solve Tommy's murder."

"I'm not going to turn you in for killing murderers."

Dr. Menzer has aided me too, by not saying anything about the X-rays, and hopefully Morgan will come around as well. Though she was pretty shaken. But if she were to turn me in? The info would go straight to my father, and he'll cover it up as he has all along. But right now I can't decide if that's a good or bad thing.

But now Travis's father knows. The only other person in town who is arguably more powerful than my father. And who knows what he'll do with this information?

Finally my dad speaks again, and his words are weighed, like he's effectively gathered his thoughts.

"Traumatic things have a way of coming to you when your body's ready to handle them," he says, then takes a deep breath. "Your brain couldn't handle what it was experiencing. Forcing you to face things you couldn't even process could've made you worse. Cause more blackouts, more sleepwalking episodes. So I left you alone, hoping it would stop after you finally avenged Billy Engel's and your mother's deaths."

"Travis and Travis's father."

"Yes."

"Why did he kill her?"

With this, he leans forward. He looks more sad and serious than I've ever seen.

"I don't know."

Travis's father has covered his tracks so well he's left no proof for my dad to find. We agree that the best way for us to get attribution is to work together. But we need to find out why Travis's dad set up a fake drive-by of which I was, apparently, the only living witness. So we need to unlock my memories so we can put the pieces together.

My father isn't happy with that idea. He didn't want me to go to therapy in the first place. I have a sleeping murderer buried inside me under only a thin, flimsy, subconscious barrier.

Poor Mrs. Lane. She had no idea what would come out when she put me under hypnosis. She was probably only ready for stories of my father touching me in naughty places.

But since she's the only therapist I know who already has some idea of what I'm capable of, she might be the only one who can help me.

Repression

Needless to say, Mrs. Lane isn't thrilled when my father and I appear at her office.

"I told you I wouldn't tell anyone, Sherriff Janus," Mrs. Lane says flatly. "But I'm prepared to file a restraining order," she adds, eyeing me heavily.

"That won't be necessary," my father insists. "My daughter really needs your help."

"Clearly," she huffs at the understatement.

"I'm stronger than I look," my father says. And the uniform sells it. "I'll stay in the room and protect you from her if it's necessary, but I promise you it won't be. She only kills murderers."

"Murderers," Mrs. Lane repeats, with her eyes far away. "That's why she said that."

"Said what?" I jump on her comment, and she lurches backwards in her chair, like she thinks I'll physically pounce on her. Then she composes herself.

"You asked me if I was one."

"I did?"

"And I said, 'No, I'm a therapist.'"

"And what did I say?"

"You said, 'I don't come out for therapists. You must be a

lousy one.'"

It's probably insensitive that my dad and I both burst out laughing simultaneously, but it's just so funny. But when we see her horrified expression, we both cut off practically simultaneously as well.

"How...rude of *her*," I say awkwardly, not really sure which pronoun is correct. She winces through my false apology. "I think you're a great therapist," I lie as best I can, but it comes out completely unconvincing so I just get to the point. "And I need you to hypnotize me again so we can retrieve those memories."

"There might be a good reason they're buried," she says, lighting a cigarette she's brought out from her pocket with a match and sucking it down nervously. "They might need to stay there." She waves out the match with a hiss at an accidentally burned finger.

This from a therapist? I have to admit this scares me a little. She thinks my memories are worse than any retrieved from her other patients, and she's probably right, but I know the key to solving the "why" of my mother's murder is in there and this is the only way to find it.

"My mother was murdered," I say.

"By you?" she jumps on me a little bravely considering

what she's seen. I'm starting to get a little angry, and my dad sees it. I feel like getting in her face and asking her to say that again, but my dad puts a crushing hand on my shoulder.

"No," he informs her. "I suspect she was there when it happened though, and we need to know everything about that night so we can find who did it. This is an unsolved case from a while back."

"Seems like several of your cases have turned out that way, like the murders or disappearances of almost everyone accused of killing Billy Engel?"

"That's true," my dad admits. "But do you really have an issue with those disappearances going unsolved? I can assure you that each and every one of those boys is guilty."

"No," she admits, which is more than I could've hoped for. Never pinned her as a capital punishment type. You'd think she'd want those boys in here to share their feelings, drink soothing tea and hit each other with foam bats or something.

"Okay, so can you help her, please?" my father begs, and it's the only time I've ever seen him do this. "It's not healthy for her to live like this."

She weighs this truth in her head, and it's apparent she agrees.

"Lie down, Kalana."

It isn't long before I'm relaxing into her silly, airy, far-away voice: "You're heavy...you're relaxed...you're weightless."

Soon the tunnel surrounding the pinpoint of light appears, and since I told her about it beforehand, she tries guiding me through it this time: "Now you're in a long, dark tunnel, and instead of retreating, you're going to walk toward the pinpoint of light."

Somehow my mind obeys even though I feel like this tactic is totally stupid. I move toward the bright light and see the room I'm in with her sitting over me as I lay on the, now *blue*, couch. (She must've thrown out the white one stained with my blood.)

I'm detached again and hanging over the present moment watching myself sleep. I look peaceful enough. But then the heat and nausea strike me again and, from the corner, my consciousness watches my own eyes flip open. They're fully black. Mrs. Lane stands and moves away. My dad draws closer.

I stand and throw my arms to my sides like they're weapons themselves, and the white, blood-covered bones rip through the flesh of my recently stitched wrists and extend out into the room. They span from wrists to high above my forehead, surrounding and embracing my upper body like a protective ring of blood and bones. My face shows no sign of the pain this must've caused. Is this what it really looks like, or am I just imagining it this way? Are my bone-knives really this extensive? I'm staring right into the therapist's eyes coldly, trying to determine if she was the reason I was brought out.

"You again," I/she says in that sinister, airy voice. "You're no murderer."

"No," Mrs. Lane managers to squeak out. She's truly terrified, and I can't help finding that funny from where my detached, projected consciousness floats in the top corner of the room. "Kalana asked me to bring you out because she wants the memories you're keeping from her."

She/I laughs and eyes me, the projected consciousness that thinks I'm/she's floating instead of inside that body right now saying these things.

"She's doesn't want them," the me—that isn't exactly me—claims. "They're horrific."

"She does," Mrs. Lane insists. "She needs to solve your mother's murder."

She/I laughs again and looks up at me. "Are you sure?" she asks me. Or I ask myself? Whatever. I just nod.

She/I faints, and I'm back in my body when our back

collides with the plush blue couch.

And the memories move into the parts of my brain they once vacated, filling in blanks, slowly. One memory fills in at a time, but backwards. The most recent strikes first.

I'm standing in the gym after seeing Rodney and Travis in position to attempt the act of raping Morgan. I feel sick and hot, and something in my brain snaps. Then I feel this blissful release of power, sureness and a complete absence of fear. The bone-knives rip through my recently stitched and pink flesh painlessly and expand out in front of me, like wings of bones surrounding my shoulders and head like a large bloody halo.

Then I smile into Rodney and Travis's horrified faces, feel a little bit of regret at Morgan's fear and step toward Rodney, the closer one.

One step and the spinning five-point bone-knives at the end of my bone-chains shred him into chunks of blood, spliced organs and black and white fabric. He's gone before he can scream.

But Travis moves quickly and manages to escape through the emergency exit. Not that I'm concerned. There's no escaping me. He will meet his end soon enough.

With one last look at the expressions of Morgan, Tobias and Eddie—all surprised except Eddie—I pass out, and that memory ends.

A new one follows on its heels.

I get out of my bed and walk to school in the dark with my head hung, not awake or asleep, so the memory of the trip is vague, but once I get to the cafeteria, I look through the window from the hall and see Tommy Mitchell standing over Eddie Sherman kicking him in the gut over and over. I enter the room, and my rage awakens.

Tommy looks terrified of me even before the knives expand out. It must be that horrifying expression of rage twisting my features.

He steps away from Eddie, who's bleeding and gasping on the tile floor, and backs away from me as I approach. The knives rip through my flesh and barely display themselves—rendering me a terrifying, reverse-winged angel—before they tear through him.

I leave a very bloody mess and a confused Eddie. All he can say is my name, with a lingering question at the end.

I fall back half-asleep and walk home, get into bed and sleep soundly.

The next memory is a little further back. It involves happening upon Nurse Roberts and her son at the playground right when Nurse Roberts is struggling with someone in the dark.

When the street light hits him, it's Preston Owen. He's shushing her. Tells her everything will be alright. If she just lets him have it in front of her son and if her son doesn't cry during, he won't hurt them.

They both agree out of desperation, and that infuriates me at their attacker. When I step forward, I snap a branch on the ground, and he notices me, smirks and says, "Hi there, girl. Want to join in?"

I feel the satisfying release and a sly smile hits my lips.

"Yesssss," I hiss.

When the light hits me, recognition and fear consume him. He lets go of Nurse Roberts, who runs to her boy's side.

"Oh shit. It's you," he says, strangely. My conscious mind doesn't yet understand what he means, but I have an idea I will, especially since I feel myself nod.

And I release the sharp bones.

The little boy falls backwards in fear, and Nurse Roberts goes down with him, holding him in a reassuring bear hug.

"Don't worry, little one," she says into his ear. "She's an angel sent to save us. Remember Dante's Inferno? Angels are actually terrifying," she assures him. But I can tell from her horrified expression that she's not as confident of this as she sounds. She's just being a mom. The little boy nods and tries to believe her but won't take his eyes from me.

"You're right," I tell her. Her fear makes me nauseated, and I want her to know it isn't necessary. "Don't let him watch," I order her. She nods and covers the little boy's eyes.

But Preston's already running, not that it's hard for me to catch him in just a few strides...and pulverize him.

I stare at the bloody heap with satisfaction and then turn back to the boy and his mother. The boy still watches me carefully but the mother begins that stare of admiration.

I pass out again, my thirst for vengeance slaked once again.

I don't know how Mrs. Roberts cleaned up that mess with her son present. Maybe she took him home and returned, but it wasn't there the next morning.

My father looked into it since I told him what I saw on the way to the emergency center, but he never found anything. Mrs. Roberts wiped that mess out of existence. She did it to save me. And she's never said a word about that evening to anyone, barely even to me.

The second to last memory floods in. I'm sleepwalking again, and it's when I'm swaying by the school parking lot that I hear the sounds of some very cruel teasing.

It's Billy Engel hollering about wanting his toy cars back while a group of five boys surround him, tossing him around like a ragdoll as they take turns crushing his cars under their feet, holding him and landing very hard punches to his jaw and kicks to his head.

I run toward them, but I'm a football field away when I start. Before I can get there, Travis has taken a golf club out of the back of his truck.

He says, "Do you think if we hit you in the head enough we can fix you?"

Billy cries and screams for him to stop, but Travis strikes him hard and Billy goes down. Then he passes the golf club around, and they all take a swing, even though Billy hasn't moved or made a sound since the first blow.

That's when I arrive. Travis, Rodney and Tommy take off without a word to leave their two friends standing over the body. Since I'm untouched by the parking lot light they stand under, they can't tell who I am. Nausea, heat, disgust. My true form emerges for only the second time. That's when Preston runs. He was always nervous around me until the day he met a similar end. He no doubt warned Travis and Rodney about me, but they didn't believe him until they saw for themselves.

The boy who stays behind, Blaine Spencer, is frozen by my terrible beauty. He doesn't dare move while uselessly hoping I'll spare him. He wants mercy when he's shown none. He even tries to bargain with me. "We're sorry. *I'm* sorry," he says. "We're not bad people," he claims. "It just got out of hand."

No.

"Muurdddeeerer," I slur, and he backs away from me, but it's already too late. I slice through his bewildered and frozen face, which is screwed up into one last expression of terror.

Then I wander home covered in blood, and that's when my father finds me before I crawl into bed.

"They killed Billy Engel," I tell him.

"Who?"

I list them. He asks me where.

"The school," I say and then pass out on the bed. He wakes me, quickly drops me off at the emergency room and, I assume, goes back to clean up the shredded body. Then he supposedly discovers Billy Engel's body on a routine patrol while Blaine's body never surfaced, but his prints were the freshest on Travis' golf club so he was presumed the murderer and suspected to have fled the country. Though all five of the boys' prints were found on the golf club, they all denied it and had good lawyers. Even Travis, who owned the driver, claimed that Blaine borrowed it, even though it was he who took the first swing.

It all makes sense. I destroyed one of them on the spot and left the other four for the next time they tried to hurt someone, knowing it was inevitable.

But I feel my hand grab at the couch cushion of plush beneath me as I get ready for the last, missing memory. The one I assume is the most painful because it started all of this.

It hits me with a surge of pain when it starts just because it's the first time I've seen my mother's face in two years. And she's smiling at me since I've just walked in the door after school. Just seeing her happy, kind face barely lined with stress, is best described as blissful pain.

I feel the tears slip down my face as I continue to follow the lost memory.

She's not alone. I hear a distressed male voice in the other room who talks as he follows her into the living room.

"How can you want to be with *that man*? Do you even realize all the things I can offer—" When he walks into the room, I easily see it's Travis's father, Mr. Malone, and he cuts off when he sees me, guiltily.

"Hello, Kalana," he says, like my name tastes bad.

"You need to leave now," my mother snaps at him. I've never heard that cutting tone in her voice before. "And stop showing up here," she demands. "Like I've said every time, I don't want *anything* you have to offer."

Mr. Malone is enraged. "You just made the biggest mistake of your life," he claims. "No one says no to me. This was your last chance." Then he leaves, phone in hand, fingers dialing.

I turn to my mom, completely flabbergasted. "What did he want?" I ask, though deep down I kind of know. I'm just politely misunderstanding so she has a chance to explain.

"Nothing you need to worry about," my mother claims and then turns to leave the room.

I'm about to follow her from the living room when we hear the screeching of tires, drunken cheering and the sound of an overzealous stereo bass.

As bullets and feathers fly, my mom turns to me, puts her back to the window and surrounds me with her arms as she drags us both to the ground.

As the deafening pops continue, I feel that overwhelming feeling of nausea and anger. The bones break free of my wrists, ripping through the unblemished skin for the first time and surrounding my mom and I in a terrifying, bloody embrace.

As the five pointed ends spin away bullets, both our faces are horrified and intrigued by this, until my mom's face has no expression at all. The bullets end, and the car screeches around the corner. My mom's arms no longer hold me, and she falls on her back, bloody. Her eyes now dim. There are bullets through her chest and head, but none in me.

I look at the strange bones expanded from my arms, covered in my blood, feel a strange surge of power and run out the door after the car, its sounds still audible in the distance. I run faster than I expect, but I can't keep up with the sounds. But even still, I run in the direction of the last place I heard the sounds of the car.

Then I'm just running aimlessly, only imagining I hear the sounds of that car and not some other. Then exhaustion takes me, and I drop to my knees and do a faceplant into someone's lush lawn.

Later that night, someone discovered me (face-down and bleeding), while rolling out their trash can, and called an ambulance.

I woke up at the emergency center with Nurse Roberts, Dr. Menzer and my father standing over me. I had no memory of that evening after school let out. I don't even remember walking home. So they all assumed I must've passed out along the way. But where I was found was nowhere near my usual walking route, and my dad already had darker suspicions. It was then, when I was barely conscious, that he told me my mother had been killed that night in a drive-by.

I wake for real in Mrs. Lane's office with my dad standing over me concerned and expectant. I stand immediately, ignoring my bleeding wrists. It's starting to feel like my natural waking state.

"He was in love with her," I tell my dad with a shaky voice. "And she said no. So he *killed* her." I can barely get those words out. They're so disgusting to me.

The pain in my dad's face makes my stomach churn. "Only monsters love like that," he says under his breath in an anger-coated voice I've never heard from him before. I start to see a veil come over his eyes. They seem to get darker and angrier every second.

Am I imagining this?

But before I can decide, goons wearing gas masks burst into the office, shoot Mrs. Lane in the head with a silenced bullet and gas my dad and I so that we pass out before either of us can release our rage.

In the Dark

I wake up in chains, suspended from the ceiling of some dank warehouse, next to my dad, who's also chained but not yet awake. There's a bare bulb above us, and we're the only things illuminated by its light.

I'm still bleeding from my wrists, and it's pooling on the floor beneath me. I also feel lightheaded with a hard headache. I need to get to Dr. Menzer soon, or I'm going to die.

"Dad," I hiss at him as quietly as I can, but he doesn't answer. There are other figures in this dark expansive room, five or so, talking low, but I can't make them out in the dark. Then one of them steps into the light—Travis's father, Mr. Malone.

"My son tells me you killed all his friends," he says to me. My dad jerks awake in reaction to Mr. Malone's voice and quickly takes in our dire predicament. I watch him examine the chain links, looking for a weak one to break.

"He wants me to kill you," Mr. Malone continues, addressing only me.

My dad starts working his wrists and tugging on his chains hard. He's decided the weakest part is where the chains are suspended by a large hook in the ceiling. He's so strong; it won't take long to yank out that hook.

"Mr. Janus, if you so much as get a hand free, my men will put a bullet in your skull," Mr. Malone warns. My dad stops his struggle, but his expression is that of a steadily growing fury.

"But I don't want to kill you, Kalana," Mr. Malone continues. "Power like that should be harnessed."

My head starts to sink forward. I've lost too much blood, but my dad's voice brings me back temporarily.

"You can't harness pure rage," he tells Mr. Malone.

"Oh, can't I?" Mr. Malone asks. "What sets you off, Kalana? Is it anger?"

I wake up again when Mr. Malone addresses me, but then I slip again, my head dropped forward.

"I think we can arrange that," I hear Mr. Malone say, but his voice is slow, echo-y and far away. "Boys, put a bullet in Mr. Janus's head."

No! When I hear that, I struggle to wake but can't. I'm too deep under, and I've lost too much blood. Daddy!

"Oh, so all your men are murderers just like you," Dad says strangely. I can tell he's stalling, but I don't understand why he chose those words so deliberately, until I feel myself whisper the word "Muuurrrddderers" unintentionally in my passed-out state. The other one is coming out.

"Murderer is such a naked term," Mr. Malone claims. "I prefer innovators."

"So it *was* your boys that killed my wife."

"Of course," Mr. Malone said. "You were making Haven so safe, you were driving out all my business." Then he adds with a laugh, "No one really stays at Haven hotel."

Even in my slipping state, I can't believe Dad's ridiculous theory was right.

"So that's really it. You really just killed her to warn me away. That and the whole 'she rejected you' thing," my father takes pleasure in saying.

Mr. Malone is silent. I can feel his anger and wounded pride, but he doesn't speak to it.

"I wanted to hurt *you*," he clarifies when he finally responds. "I was even thrilled when I realized your daughter was going to be home when it happened. In fact, I was there when she came home from school that day. Didn't your wife ever tell you about all my visits during the day while you were at work?"

"No, but I suspect she was just trying to keep me from beating you to death and ending up in jail," Dad also takes pleasure in saying.

That certainly sounds like mom. But Mr. Malone ignores

the ease at which Dad answers his question and continues.

"I thought it was strange that Kalana escaped but didn't seem to know anything about what happened. I assumed she repressed it, but I never imagined she would turn out to be this special. I should've known there was something about her when everyone I sent after the two of you a while back kept disappearing...before I gave up." (What does he mean? I have no memory of killing anyone else.) "And we're about to see how special. Boys? The Bullet? Mr. Janus's head?"

No!

A bullet sounds out from the dark just as the bone-knives extend through my pre-ripped flesh. One vector fans out in front of my dad's forehead so quickly it takes a minute for my brain to catch up. Did I deflect the bullet? God, tell me I saved him! My dad looks startled by the scary, bloody bones collected so near his face.

But there's blood all over his forehead.

It's mine.

The small bullet is clasped tightly between two of the knife-points in the five-point fan of bone. I didn't deflect the bullet. I *caught* it.

The men start to fire at us both without instruction.

My fan-knives spin and deflect the multiple bullets from

their guns, mostly back into the bodies of the people who shot them, until they're all out of ammo and some are collapsed over.

Neither my dad nor I are touched. During my deflections, my dad successfully ripped both sets of chains and hooks out of the ceiling. From there, it's easy for him to rip and crush the chains free of our bodies. They break between his clutches like clay.

Then Dad gets really mad.

"You shoot at my daughter?" he screams at all of them, but then he's directing it solely at Mr. Malone, who's regrettably unscathed. "YOU. SHOOT. AT. MY. DAUGHTER?"

The two of the four men that aren't gut-shot rush him, but I shred them before they can even land one punch on my dad. And he just follows after the fleeing Mr. Malone with laser focus.

I know I'm being hypocritical, especially right now when I've totally boiled over myself...and just shredded two more people...yet am somehow remaining self-aware, *strange*. But I suddenly can't decide if the surfacing of my dad's true anger is a good or bad thing. His features have contorted into an arrangement of rage I've never seen on his face, and his eyes have gone completely...black.

Jesus. My eyes really do that? I thought that was just how I imagined myself. Is this what I really look like when I lose it?

Mr. Malone tries to run but slips on a pool of blood next to one of his dying men.

Then Dad screams in a full-throated, deep screech of pain that's truly unnerving, even to me in my current state.

I back away from him, not wanting to be near when whatever's about to happen, happens. But when doing this, I unintentionally step on a gut-shot goon who grabs my foot and digs in his nails around my Achilles tendon, meaning to sever it.

But without taking my eyes off my dad, or much thought, I send one of my vectors to rip out his throat.

Then my dad's arms erupt at the wrist with a splash of blood. Out extend two long bones, the length of my dad's forearms, blood-covered and solid. They look like enormous billy clubs, stowed away inside him.

Oh my God.

My dad drops to one knee beside Mr. Malone and starts beating him mercilessly while he screams at him with each slug.

"YOU. SHOT. AT. MY. DAUGHTER?"

"YOU. KILL. MY. WIFE?"

The blood pooling around Mr. Malone's head seems endless.

"THIS. IS. MY. TOWN!"

"THIS. ISN'T. YOUR. TOWN. ANY—"

Crunch.

That was Mr. Malone's skull caving in.

The blackness slowly fades from my father's eyes as he awkwardly climbs to his feet, looking tired but not necessarily confused. I think he somehow retained his awareness as well. Like me, he had a rage blackout without the blackout.

His bone batons pull back inside and the only things left to show for them are quarter-sized punctures at the wrist that aren't bleeding a dangerous amount.

That's why his aren't obvious like mine. They don't make as big a hole. A scar there would be easier to hide and it would heal faster, and since I've seen my dad's wrists exposed often for the last two years with no fresh scars, I suspect they haven't come out in a while. Probably not since he, apparently, killed a string of Mr. Malone's goons sent to stop him from cleaning up the town. Goons that Mr. Malone mistakenly thought I took care of. And before that, probably not since he beat two muggers half to death five years ago.

The report did say the beatings were so severe they suspected a weapon must have been involved. But none was ever found.

But I'm a little angry at my father for his omission, especially when I've been struggling so hard with this "gift."

"You said you didn't have anything in your arms," I object as I approach him cautiously, though his eyes have already unblacked.

"I said I didn't have any *knives*," he corrects me.

So he did. Still shitty not to mention it. I guess he hoped they'd never come out again. Maybe after today, they won't.

"I get why you don't bother carrying a billy club now," I say with a laugh. He laughs too, but then his face weighs down with concern.

"Kalana," he says seriously, "I'm sorry you had to see that side of me."

"I'm not," I say easily, still pretty whacked out with my blood-covered bone-wings extended from my arms and, most likely, black eyes. And I don't just say it because it's hypocritical not to. Seeing him that way is pretty amazing. I wonder if it's kind of awesome to watch me.

I'll have to take a survey later. I turn to the last person bleeding on the floor. I originally thought he was a goon but spotted him from across the room a second ago, bleeding profusely, and saved him for last.

It's Travis. No doubt watching his father's way of conducting business so he can take over one day. Or possibly waiting for his chance to kill me when his father's back was turned. Well, he's certainly no threat now, not that he even was before.

I kneel beside him, and put my black eyes close to his brown, soulless ones.

"You murdered Billy Engel," I hiss. He shakes his head. His whole body is riddled with tremors. He's dying already. One bullet to each lung.

"We were just playing," he manages to force out of his blood-gushing mouth.

"Well, *I'm* not playing."

"Please. Have mercy," he sputters, bloodily.

"Why should I when you didn't?"

"You're right. You're right," he gasps desperately. "But—"

"No mercy for the wicked," I hiss.

When I watch my bone-knives cut through his being, it's like I'm watching it in slow motion. They crack through his finely chiseled jaw, cut through his perfectly straight nose, slice out his porcelain-capped teeth and gash through his gym-sculpted body like I'm cutting through a flesh-colored cake with a velvet filling. I smile when I stand over the leftovers, which I've cut so finely they look like the remains of nothing in particular. He's reduced to a

pile of bloody chunks.

I feel my smile as I retract my bone-knives and collapse.

Blood loss.

Almost Dead

Dr. Menzer wakes me to say that I really *really* almost died this time, as opposed to the *really* almost died he claimed the last time.

I guess I don't take him as seriously as I should. I feel indestructible right now, but he keeps telling me I will really really *really* die next time if I don't get myself here pronto after once again falling on a pair of magically elusive knives.

He's also noticeably irritated with my dad as he stitches him up second. (He lost much less blood.)

"I thought you, at least, knew better than this," he says to my dad with a grimace.

"I do normally," my dad says guiltily, eyes downcast.

I guess, also inside Dr. Menzer's safe, is a secret X-ray of my dad's bone batons hidden inside his forearms. Dr. Menzer seems to know more about us than I would've ever guessed, despite his preference to know as little as possible.

"It's one thing to let your daughter play with knives repeatedly, but to play with knives together?" Dr. Menzer says without even attempting to check his sarcasm. "That's just irresponsible parenting."

"Absolutely," my dad says with a laugh. "Sorry."

"Well, I guess that's all I can do for now," Dr. Menzer says when he's done stitching up my dad. "I have other patients to see now—sane ones."

Then he leaves, but not without the usual "Keep it clean" shouted over his shoulder.

But there is one addition before he goes to his next appointment. He turns to us, looks us both in the eye and says, "Like you keep our streets."

Apparently on our way to the emergency center, my dad made an anonymous call from a burner phone to the police to report screaming in the old abandoned warehouse (even though it's too far away from anywhere for anyone to hear screaming).

His men showed up and found the bodies and called him in just as Dr. Menzer was stitching up his wrists. He arrived after I was safely in bed to file a report that suggested the elusive "shredder" had gotten Mr. Malone, his son and his work associates for a shady business deal gone wrong. When all this was printed in the paper, he made sure they also printed his theory that this elusive killer was probably still gunning for any remaining Malone associates.

A New Reality

I spend the next few days in bed pretending I need the time to heal physically, when really it's my consciousness that needs to absorb all this new and strange information.

My dad seems to understand and plays along. He brings me chicken soup twice a day but otherwise leaves me alone to lie in bed and watch TV. But no amount of mindless entertainment can shield me from my thoughts.

I've killed five people. Boys. Sure, they were murderers, but so am I. How does that make me any better than them? Though I do have to admit I feel a pretty defined difference between beating a mentally handicapped person to death and killing the ones who murdered him and tried to rape my friend and Mrs. Roberts.

But I still can't stop the guilt from piling up in my stomach and threatening to choke me. I stare at my television catatonically while struggling with right and wrong, life and death and all manners of dichotomies.

And why did Tobias have to be there? Why did he have to see my true and ugly nature? I never wanted him to see that. Maybe that's why, deep down, I avoided him. I didn't want him to see the real me.

A while later, the doorbell rings, but I don't hear my dad moving to answer it. (He must be in the backyard.) So I pull myself from the bed. It's physically easy though I'm disappointed to miss the next line of the sitcom I'm watching to answer the door.

I'm shocked to see Tobias standing on the slab of concrete just before my doorstep, having only a little difficulty giving me his usual warm smile.

"Tobias, what are you doing here?" I ask through the screen door, somewhat afraid to remove the barrier.

"I came to see if you were alright."

"Me?" I ask, slapping open the door and holding it open with one hip. "You're the one who had to clean up..." I whisper the rest, "a murder scene."

"And I'd do it again," Tobias claims, holding my eyes seriously. "You think I haven't thought about taking down the ones who mercilessly killed my brother *myself*?"

I'm surprised to hear him say that, since he's good and all about forgiveness, but I guess forgiveness can only go so far. Evil is evil.

"Well, of course, but it's one thing to talk about it. It's another to actually do it."

"No, it's one thing for *me* to do it," he says, stepping onto the doorstep so his lips shamelessly linger right above mine. (I can't help noticing these things.) "But I suspect the rules are different for you."

"Why?" I ask, cross-armed and feeling naked even though I'm completely clothed and actually wearing some puffy, embarrassing pajama bottoms with elephants on them.

"I don't really think you're human," he says easily. It bothers me a little to hear him say that out loud. Makes me feel like a freak for one, but it's also incessantly been crossing my mind for the last two days; I was in comfortable denial until someone actually said it. I don't think me, or my dad, really fit into the "human" category.

"Oh, so you, just like Nurse Roberts, see my true form and think I'm some kind of scary angel?" I ask, sounding more offended than I feel. It's not the worst thing to be called.

"I was thinking something more like Wolverine," he says. "Though possibly slightly darker and without the spandex."

I know he wants me to laugh, but I can't. This isn't something to joke about.

"I'm dangerous, Tobias," I tell him, now more serious than ever.

"Not to me," he says with a nonchalant shrug.

"We don't know that for sure."

"I *do*," he says with so much assurance I want to believe him.

My dad has seen me come out more than once, and he's told others, with total confidence, that I only kill murderers. And I did leave Mrs. Lane unscathed both times the less-pleasant me surfaced in her presence.

Maybe it's true. Besides, would I ever really hurt Dad or Tobias or Morgan? Looking into his light-filled eyes, I have a stronger sense of my answer than I ever would've guessed.

No.

"But I do think you should seriously consider anger management," Tobias jokes dryly.

I can't help laughing at such an understatement. Can you imagine how much I'd terrify *that* support group? They'd wet themselves. I don't think it would remotely work, but it does sound somewhat entertaining. Huh.

"Why do you do that?" I ask, an uninvited smile breaking through my impassive mask.

"What?"

"Always accept me no matter what I do?"

"Because you deserve to be forgiven," Tobias says. Then he

moves closer than I expect. His face is inches from mine now.

"Kalana, I don't know what you are, but I know you're good. I'll never leave you."

My cheeks grow hot. How can he say these impossibly wonderful things? How can he think I deserve them? I murdered someone in front of him, and he stands over me saying he'll never leave, when I avoided him for a whole year because his brother died and it was awkward. I don't deserve this. I don't deserve him.

But instead of vocalizing any of this, I just kiss him. Some things aren't to be understood. Some things you just appreciate without question. Some things just *are*.

On my third "sick day," I run through all the sitcoms of the day, though I barely pay attention. I'm still high on Tobias kiss-age, until I notice that I've been switching between a multitude of news programs for the last 10 minutes. They all seem to focus on the same types of stories (sad, horrid stories that no one should have to hear about the murders of spouses, family, friends...children), and the same city names seem to come up over and over again. It's truly depressing.

My eyes are glued to all the horrible depictions when my dad comes in with a lap-table and puts a steaming bowl of soup under my nose.

"What are you thinking so hard about?" Dad asks.

"Where I'm going to live after I graduate," I say, feeling my wicked smile before it erupts on my face. "Did you know that New Orleans still has one of the highest murder rates in the nation?"

My dad laughs but cuts off quickly, instantly thinking better of his natural reaction. "Well...finish with Haven High first and then...we'll talk," he claims, handing me a napkin and a spoon.

Back to School

When I return to school, I'm afraid it'll take Morgan some time to be comfortable talking to me after seeing me shred Rodney, even in protection of her. But she sits down right next to me during English and gives a forced but sincere smile.

"I've decided you are an angel of God," she tells me without hesitation, thankfully in a code only she and I understand.

"Really?" I ask, stunned. Morgan isn't the type to be a fan of retribution.

"Yeah. I mean. I don't really approve of your methods. But if you hadn't have helped me when you did, think of where I'd be," she points out.

True. I'm glad she didn't have to experience that kind of intrusive torture. No one should have to.

"Yeah," I say, not able to string anything more together than a one-word response. I'm stunned by her about-face. She's somehow okay with this after she saw what I am? Not that I'm not secretly annoyed she ditched me when I could've used her help getting to the emergency room. I guess me skipping half the school week gave her time to think. But still. I didn't expect her to come around this fast, or honestly, at all.

"And don't worry," Morgan says, adding with a whisper. "I

won't tell anyone."

I consider this for a moment and quickly form a plan I wish I'd thought of sooner. If I had, I probably would've returned to school on Monday instead of lying low.

"Oh no, Morgan," I tell her with a calculated heaviness to my words. "I want you to tell *everyone*."

By the end of the school year, the rumors circulating throughout the school that revolve around me go like this: Kalana Janus is a witch, bloodletter and possibly a vampire. She had a series of rage blackouts and killed all the boys who beat Billy Engel to death with a golf club: Tommy Mitchell, Preston Owen, Blaine Spencer, Rodney Chutney and Travis Malone. She also killed Travis' father because it turns out he was the one responsible for her mother's death. The police, namely her sheriff father, cover up her actions because they condone them, which is why she's never been caught. She also supposedly has giant bone-knives inside her arms that cut through her skin and rip people to shreds. She is possibly also a hell angel sent here to destroy evil people.

Few really believe all these rumors. But Haven has never been safer.

June 17, 2016
Report of Terrorists on Flight Instantly Redacted
Associated Press

NEW ORLEANS—Today there was a distress call from the cellular phone of a passenger inside a plane bathroom. This eyewitness aboard flight 3427 from DFW reported seeing terrorists with bombs threatening to kill women and children if anyone thwarted their attempt to bring down the plane. Fifteen minutes later, the same passenger called to report that he was mistaken. There were no terrorists.

This was further confirmed when the plane landed and was boarded by Homeland Security. Upon searching the plane, they found no evidence of terrorists or explosives. However, one woman—covered, allegedly, in her own blood—was instantly rushed off the plane to an undisclosed hospital, where she was treated for ruptured wrists. Apparently, she had fainted and fell on a pair of sharp objects; however, none of the other passengers witnessed this bizarre accident and no sharp objects were recovered from the plane. Even the woman's husband, who was traveling with her, claimed that he "didn't see what happened." In fact, many of the passengers, some without even being asked, claimed that they "didn't see anything."

New Orleans officials say they are perplexed by this unprecedented case of mistaken terrorism, but as recently hired Orleans Parish Sheriff Robert Janus said, "It certainly could've been worse. I say we take this one as a win."

The identity of this woman was not released by officials, allegedly because she was undergoing medical treatment at press time.

See the following excerpt from the second book in the *Periphery*

Series.

Coming Soon....

Bloodless

By Kelly E. Lindner

Blood Traces

They told me they were taking me to the hospital, but that doesn't seem to be where I am. Even in my half-awake state, I can tell something is different. They're treating my wounds differently to begin with. Instead of the usual tugging of stitches through my skin, there's the smell of burning flesh and a strange metallic taste in my mouth. There's also this unusual sensation in my arms. They feel like they're being simultaneously emptied and filled at the same time. It doesn't make sense.

When I wake, I'm sitting in a chair in an empty room except for a long table with another person at the end of it—a black-haired man wearing a suit. Each of my wrists is handcuffed to a chair arm, and my forearms feel *heavier*. Even without the handcuffs, I'm not sure I could easily lift them in my weakened state. I look down at them to see *not* bandages but these black cloth bands stretching from wrists to elbows. When I look back to the man, I don't even try to struggle. I just ask, "What do you want?" I sound groggier than I expect.

"Kalana Janus," he says my name like it tastes bad. I'm tired of people saying my name that way.

"It's Engel, actually," I correct him. Then I have a horrible thought, and my face whitens. "Where's Tobias?"

"He's safe," he assures me with the wave of his hand. It's so dismissive I believe him.

Then he continues. "Do you have any idea how hard what you just did was to clean up?"

"*What?*" I ask.

"There were bits of terrorist all over that plane and *you.* Even after a good washing, blood leaves traces. That might've worked in Haven where your dad was the only law but *on a plane?* We had to change those flight records to subtract those two people you shredded. And dispose of their remains once we pumped the plane's septic tank. Even if your father is now the Sheriff of Orleans Parish—how *convenient* by the way—you created a lot of work for us."

I start wondering who "us" is: Homeland Security? FBI? CIA? But I suspect he won't tell me so I just ask, "Why would you clean it up?"

"Oh don't get me wrong, Mrs. *Engel.* You did a good thing. It's just how you went about it that we have a problem with."

"Is there a better way?" I ask, confused and a little irritated.

"Oh yes," he says, a strange smile spreading on his lips.

"And we'd be happy to show you."

"Who's *we*?" I ask but suspect it's fruitless. He's probably trained not to answer that question. But he surprises me by saying, "A government agency," though it's vague. "But not one you've ever heard of," he adds.

Then he presses a button on a little remote control so that a door behind him swings open. Next a group of five people walk in, all dressed in black. It's a collection of men and women who are all different sizes and shapes. It's not the lineup you'd expect from the FBI or the CIA. They look like completely normal people, except a very large man on one end who is built like a wrestler.

But they all have these strange black bands stretching from their elbows to their wrists, just like what's currently on each of my arms. I glance down and wish I could peel them back and see what's underneath, but I'm still cuffed.

"Show her," the man says to the group. Simultaneously they each pull the black bands from their forearms, and there's this strange contraption built into each of their arms. It's like a metal chamber that's open on the top so whatever's inside can come out without ripping through flesh. And the skin around the metal opening is cauterized.

Their eyes darken. Then they each display the extensive

bone abnormalities that are inside each of their arms in succession.

The wrestler-type on the end has what looks like maces inside his huge arms. The small woman next to him has something akin to sharp knitting needles. The one after that, machetes. The next one, a curved blade, and the last one, three-point blades, reminiscent of small tridents.

They're all different, but all *like me*. Yet they can display what's inside without blood or pain. And their formations are not bathed in blood. They're a flawless white.

I feel my completely surprised expression draw into a smile. The man in the suit seems to like my reaction. He presses another button on his remote, and my handcuffs fall free.

Then I slowly lift my heavy wrists and pull away the black band surrounding my own strange abnormalities.

There are my knives, folded-up, bone-white and clean inside an open metal chamber that's been fused with my surrounding skin. Under my control, they slowly extend free of my arms without pain. For the first time I see them as a gift instead of curse. They're truly beautiful.

And wielding them, I'll do beautiful things.